MW01488495

CLOUDS GRAY

CLOUDS GRAY

KAROL WHALEY

Clouds envelop me
Dark gray is all my eyes see
God, I need your help.

Copyright © 2017 by Karol Whaley

All rights reserved. No part of this publication may be reproduced, stored in a retrieval system, or transmitted in any form or by any means—electronic, mechanical, photo-copying, recording, or otherwise—without the prior written permission of the publisher. The only exception is brief quotations in printed reviews. For information, address Hartline Literary Agency; 123 Queenston Dr.; Pittsburgh, Pennsylvania 15235.

The characters and events in this book are fictional, and any resemblance to actual persons or events is coincidental or is a fictionalized account of an actual event.

Scripture taken from the New Century Version* ®, Copyright © 2005 by Thomas Nelson. Used by permission. All rights reserved.

Scriptures and additional materials quoted are from the Good News Bible, Copyright © 1994, published by the Bible Societies/ HarperCollins Publishers Ltd UK, Good News Bible, Copyright © American Bible Society 1966, 1971, 1976, 1992. Used with permission.

ISBN: 9781545201107

*This book is dedicated to the Lord Jesus Christ
and His beloved Japanese.*

CHAPTER ONE

The eighteen wheels of the Boeing 747 provided a smooth landing on the wet runway as it reversed thrust to slow down the aircraft. The temperature that late December night in 1993 was 32 degrees Fahrenheit, 0 degrees Celsius. The passengers saw a field of white awaiting them under the airport's floodlights. A high-humidity Sapporo snowstorm, with a continuous flow of huge snowflakes, made for a virtual holiday postcard. Eiko stared out the plane window and smiled. *It is so wonderful to be home for the holidays and to be greeted by the big snowflakes, falling slowly, majestically, until they reach their destination on the snow-covered ground. There is nothing more beautiful... or peaceful!*

After the huge plane taxied slowly, as if to allow the 400 passengers a few minutes longer to appreciate the view, it pulled up to its gate and came to a complete stop. Eiko released her seatbelt and stood to retrieve her carry-on bag from the overhead compartment. People were already starting to file out, so she joined them in the aisle for the walk through the jet-way into the Chitose Airport arrival area, where most everything was already closed down for the night.

She made her way down the escalator, through the baggage claim area, and to the arrival lobby, where friends and relatives gathered to pick up their loved ones. She searched for her older brother, Yuitsu, whom she affectionately called Yu, but didn't spot him in the crowd.

1

Inside the terminal, she found a seat next to a closed ramen shop. *Somehow he must have been delayed,* she thought. *I do not want to upset Mother by calling and asking where he is, so I will just give him thirty minutes of grace before deciding to ride a bus or the train into Sapporo.*

Yu soon showed up, with wet hair and foggy glasses, dressed in his work suit and regular shoes—no boots— right before the thirty minutes was up. She arose and went to meet him as he approached. Eiko noticed his face was flushed, and he slipped and stumbled a bit on the wet road, as they made their way to the car in the parking lot. She worried that he had been drinking after work with his coworkers.

How did he drive here in his unstable condition? How will we get back home? It is about an hour drive on the toll roads. Eiko knew her brother drank, as did most Japanese salarymen, to get approval and acceptance within the company. At her workplace in Tokyo, however, things were different because of the influence the boss's wife had on her husband. The workers were encouraged to go home to their families at night, even though some still chose to go out drinking.

"Sorry, Eiko. I had a late night with my coworkers," Yu said. "I hope you were not worried."

She laid a hand on his arm. "Yu, have you been drinking tonight?"

He shrugged. "I have had a few beers, but it has not slowed me down. I am in control."

Eiko had her doubts. "I do not think I want to ride home with you in the car. You should not drive. And you know I do not have a license."

A look of impatience flashed across Yu's face. "I got here, right? So do not worry. Besides, there is no one out on the roads tonight."

"It is Christmas Eve, Brother. Everyone is out on the roads tonight!"

He chuckled. "It will be fine. Stop worrying. Come on. Mother is waiting for us at home."

As Eiko and her brother got into the family's white, mid-sized Nissan, she wished again that she had her driver's license. But with no other options but to let Yu drive, she decided to sit in the backseat, thinking it was safer in case of an accident. She said a quiet prayer on the way home, asking Heavenly Father to guide their car safely for the next hour.

It was obvious, once their home was in sight, that Yu took pride in the fact that he got them home all in one piece. In fact, they made it home faster than they ever had before—at least, as far as Eiko could remember. However, she also knew he had occasional issues with excessive speed, which endangered them and others on the busy toll roads.

As they drove into the driveway and pulled into their carport, Eiko said a quick *"arigatou,"*—thank you—to the Lord for His traveling mercies from the airport. She was glad the porch light was on at their gray, two-story home, but the door proved to be locked. She reached into her leather purse, pulled out her own house key, and opened the door. "Mother?" she called. "Yu and I are back from the airport."

All was quiet. She noticed that most of the house lights were off, with only two left on: one in the entryway and one in the kitchen. She spotted a note on the kitchen table. Eiko picked it up and read it aloud: "I have gone to bed. See you in the morning."

Eiko looked at Yu and handed him the note. He glanced at it, wadded it up, and threw it into the nearby trash can.

Eiko drew her brows together. "Yuitsu, are you angry with Mother? What's going on inside of you? Please talk to me."

Since their father's death the previous month, their mother had become terribly depressed, not wanting to live with the knowledge that she would never see her loving husband again. Right then, as Eiko stood in their family's kitchen, waiting for Yu to answer, the realization of the depth of her mother's grief caused a deep sadness to wash over her. Eiko had returned home for the New Year's holidays, with a few extra days added on, to cheer up her mother. Now she wondered if that would be possible in such a short amount of time.

"Mother is making such a big deal of Father's death," Yu complained. "Why can she not mourn like other people and move on? It is not as if she is all alone in her grief. We each have our own grief to bear. And there are other family members who are trying to help her through this difficult time."

"Are you one of those family members, Yu?" Eiko pressed. "Have you been trying to help her?"

Her brother's dark eyes were piercing. "You know," he pleaded, "how difficult work is at this time of year. Or… maybe you do not."

"I do," Eiko assured him. "But the difference is that my company in Tokyo has a kind boss, who cares for his employees when the work is extra demanding. I do have a friend who told me her place of employment becomes a hostile environment when the demands rise. Perhaps that sums up your situation."

Yu nodded. "Yes. That is why coworkers go out drinking so often. We all carry a common burden. People can share easier when they are away from the workplace. In addition, employers sometimes want to go along by offering to pay for all the drinks. This helps them gain points with their coworkers, who cannot stay mad at them when considering their generosity."

"Is that why you were late to get me at the airport?"

His shoulders sagged. "Sorry, Eiko. I just could not say no. I had to go for at least a couple of hours."

Yu, still a little wobbly on his feet, pulled out a chair and sat down.

"How about if I fix you some herbal tea? It will make you feel better." Eiko reached for the teapot in the cupboard, not waiting for his reply. When the hot brew was ready, she brought two steaming cups to the table and sat down across from Yu. *I do not think I have seen him feel this miserable in his whole life. Lord, please give me the necessary words to encourage him.*

They sat silently for a few moments, sipping their tea. Eiko had looked up to her brother all her life. Yu was smart and kind. He had been very good at sports during his school days, especially soccer and basketball, and he was always happy to teach her some pointers to get her interested and involved, too.

"Yu, I am sorry for your pain and hurt right now," she ventured. "Jesus, I am sure, wants to help you. He is a wonderful Friend and Savior. He loves you so much. I know that for sure because I just asked Him into my heart and was baptized."

That got his attention. Yu's eyebrows shot up, and he blinked in obvious surprise. "You became a Christian, Eiko? Really? Do you realize that makes you the only Christian in our generational family tree? How selfish of you, to step away from our cultural religion. You say you are concerned about me, but I should be concerned about you. What has been going on in your life to bring this about? Why did you not tell me, your own brother? Does Mother know? Is that part of her illness?"

Eiko's eyes stung from the tears she held back. She did not expect this attack from her brother, causing a myriad of questions to race through her mind. Why couldn't he be happy for her? Would it have gone better if she had told him earlier that she had been seeking the Lord? Perhaps it was the alcohol speaking.

At last, she took a deep breath and proceeded. "I was honest with Mother, to the extent that I told her I was going to church. She was not happy, but she treated me with more respect than you have. Perhaps now is the very best time for me to be a Christian. Our family is going through a difficult period. We desperately need hope, peace, and love, all of which are gifts that Jesus Christ freely gives to those who believe in Him. He was sent into the world, not to condemn us, but to give us new life. I want our family to experience new life in Jesus Christ."

Yu stood up and walked slowly past Eiko's chair toward the sink, where he set down his empty cup. "Well, I will let you know right now that I am not interested." He left the room, and Eiko listened to his footsteps on the stairs, leading to his bedroom. *Lord, I did not mean to hurt him. I know You can do miracles. Please work miracles in Yu's heart.*

She took her cup to the sink, rinsed it and Yu's cup as well, then placed them on the counter. She turned off the kitchen light and went upstairs to her bedroom, shut the door, and let her tears flow freely until she fell asleep.

Eiko awoke the next morning to the shrill sound of the phone ringing downstairs in the living room. Waiting to see if her mother would answer it, Eiko took the opportunity to look around the room that had been hers since childhood. All the memories and trinkets of her college years were in the exact same place as before she moved to Tokyo to start her new life. She was grateful to her parents, who were concerned about her striking out on her own and yet had made the ultimate decision to let her go.

Working as an office lady in Tokyo, making new friends, and experiencing life in the big city was going well, until her papa became ill and passed away quite suddenly. Eiko had returned to her hometown briefly to attend her papa's wake and funeral, but she quickly went back to Tokyo and her work. Now, six weeks later, she was home again, this time to be with her family during the traditional New Year's holiday period.

The phone stopped ringing and she heard her mother's voice, though muffled, so she allowed herself a few more minutes to stay under her warm bed covers. Then, anxious to greet her mother and also their Siamese cat, Kiku, she got up and made her bed, dressed, and went down to the kitchen.

"*Ohayou gozaimasu.* Good morning," Eiko said as she walked to the sink where her mother, Etsuko, stood washing some fruit. They hugged briefly. "*Ogenki desu ka?* How are you today?" Eiko asked, as Etsuko put the fruit in a bowl to set on the table for breakfast.

Eiko could see her mother's sorrow, even behind her brave smile. "*Maa-maa desu.* So-so. I have had better mornings, especially the times your father and I drank coffee together before he went to work."

Eiko's heart squeezed with the pain radiating from her mother's dark eyes. "Mom, I know you must be very lonely. I am sorry that Papa was not able to wake up from his coma and join you again. I understand that…really I do. I miss Papa very much. We all do. Please let me and the rest of the family help you."

"Eiko chan, I know that. It is just that I did not have enough days to tell him how much he meant to me, how his hard work for our family was appreciated."

7

"Papa knew you cared for him," Eiko assured her mother. "Even if you never verbalized it to him, he knew."

Etsuko shook her head slowly. "Perhaps, Eiko. It has always been difficult for me to put my feelings into words. I was taught that it showed weakness if we spoke of being dependent upon someone else. Just by staying in my marriage to your father all these years conveyed the message that I was willing to serve him, right? Being there for him showed loyalty, and loyalty can be considered the same as love, can it not?"

Eiko laid her hand on her mother's shoulder. "Being loyal or faithful is one important part of love, Mom. Compassion is another part, which desires the best for someone. Love is not proud or selfish. It does not count the wrongs that have been done but always hopes that right-living and goodness will win out."

"We have never talked to each other about love before." Etsuko looked a bit confused. "Where did you learn that, Eiko?" She poured a cup of coffee for each of them and motioned for Eiko to sit down at the kitchen table with her.

"I learned about love at church," Eiko answered, as she joined her mother at the table. "Not the kind of imperfect love that people offer each other, but the love that Creator God offers us through His one and only Son, Jesus Christ. It is an awesome love, Mother, and it is available to everyone in the world. But only those who believe and trust in Jesus Christ can truly know His love ... because God is Love."

A disapproving frown preceded Etsuko's words. "Let me guess. His love does not include people who are Buddhists or Shintoists?"

"As I said, God's love includes everyone all over the world, Buddhists and Shintoists, too. But Almighty God does not allow His followers to worship other gods, so someone cannot be in Creator God's family of believers and at the same time worship Buddha's teachings or admire the sun goddess or any lesser Shinto gods. The Bible says He is a jealous God. It says in Isaiah that He is the only good God. He sent His Son, Jesus Christ, to die for our wrongdoings, even though Jesus was perfect. He died in our place, to take our punishment and to make us right with Almighty God. That means we can be friends with God."

Etsuko's eyes were fixed on Eiko as she spoke. After a brief pause, Etsuko sighed deeply and said, "So now that you are a baptized believer, a Christian, this is what you firmly believe?" Without waiting for an answer, she scooted farther back into her chair and sat with her hands in her lap. She lifted her dark eyes to the window above the sink and stared.

Eiko looked at her mother's sad appearance and paused a moment to carefully word her answer. "Mom, for several months I have been searching for meaning in my life. Sayuri, my friend at work, told me her story about how she learned of God's great love for her. I heard about our boss's wife, who loved Jesus and freely shared His love with others, including Sayuri. I learned from Masahiro, at the college retreat in the mountains, how He got to know Creator God and learned to worship Him, rather than His creations. I learned from Satoh's cousin Aki and his wife, Yoko, what Jesus' love meant to each of them before they got married, and also now that they are married. I saw these friends live their daily lives with Jesus and noticed how they had more peace and joy than those around them. It made me want Jesus in my life, too. So I apologized for my selfishness and asked Him to be my Savior and Lord." She paused a moment, but her mother continued to stare out the window. Eiko took a deep breath and went on. "His followers are like sheep, and He is the Shepherd, who always cares for them, leading them where they should go."

Eiko got up then and moved toward her mother's chair, putting her arm around her. At the same time, Kiku walked in and rubbed against Mother's legs, while purring softly. "Mom, I am asking Almighty God to comfort you during your sadness. He loves you so much! God is the one who helped me get the extra days off to spend more time with you before I have to return to Tokyo."

Etsuko smiled and nodded, then Eiko returned to her chair, pausing the conversation while they ate together in silence. After they had cleaned up the kitchen, they went into the living room and looked out the doubled-paned picture window at the freshly falling snow.

"It must be colder today, with less humidity, since the snowflakes are tiny," Eiko observed.

Etsuko nodded again. "Yes. It is colder. I heard on the news that we are supposed to get fifty-one centimeters of snow tonight. There will be lots of snow to shovel. I am glad that Hiroshi is helping me these days." She smiled. "Do you remember Hiroshi, Eiko?"

"Yes, but is he not still in junior high? How does he have time to do snow shoveling?"

"Actually, Hiroshi is already in high school. His mother thought I might need help since your papa died, so she sent him over here to ask me. He is trying to save money for a school trip, so I pay him a small fee each time he comes; that way he can put it towards his school trip. I am grateful for his help. It is too much for me to do by myself."

"I am thankful to God that He is taking care of your needs, Mother. I also want to help shovel while I am here. I remember Yu and I helped Papa when we were younger. It is hard work, even though it is fun to be outdoors."

"Yu is not around to help these days. He is nearly always away from home when I need him." Etsuko let out a long sigh and seemed to get lost in her thoughts for a few minutes. Eiko decided to give her time to work through it.

The telephone rang, and Eiko got up to go to the living room to answer it. *"Moshi moshi."*

"Hello, Eiko chan. Welcome home! This is your Uncle Kenta."

"Hello, Uncle Kenta. It is good to hear your voice." Eiko's uncle was her papa's oldest brother. He and Grandmother had visited Sapporo when her father passed away, and though it had been a sad occasion, she had been pleased to see them. "Would you like to speak to Mother?"

"Yes, please. I have some details to share with Etsuko san."

"Just a moment, please. I need to locate Mother. I believe she has gone into the kitchen." She put down the phone and soon found Etsuko in the kitchen, pouring herself another cup of coffee. "Mom, the phone is for you. It is Uncle Kenta."

Etsuko, followed by Eiko, went into the living room and picked up the phone. "Moshi moshi, Kenta san. Were you able to make your plane reservations? When can we expect you to arrive?"

After a pause, she spoke again. "Yes, certainly. December twenty-ninth to January third is perfect. By the way, I so appreciated your phone call early this morning, asking for my okay before you purchased your tickets. I am happy you both can come."

After another pause, she said, "Thank you. I appreciate your kindness. See you then." Etsuko placed the receiver back down on the phone and turned to face Eiko, who had heard everything.

"That is wonderful that Grandmother and Uncle Kenta are coming," Eiko said, as they settled back onto the couch.

"I miss Papa so much, and it makes me happy that his oldest brother and mother want to be here to help us. Families are important in times of crisis. I thank God for sending them to comfort us."

Eiko's gaze focused on the end table and a small photo of Papa's original family. Grandpa stood with Grandma in the background, and in front of them sat their three sons: Kenta, Yoshi, and Eiji, her Papa. It was sad that three family members were no longer with them—Grandpa, Yoshi, and Papa. When Uncle Kenta's wife passed away five years ago, he became Grandmother's full-time caregiver. Now it was just the two of them on Papa's side of the family.

"I was such a young bride," Etsuko confessed, picking up the photo of herself and Papa, which sat next to the family picture on the same end table. "My father was elderly and very sickly when I married your papa. And, as you know, I was an only child. Things were difficult, but your papa and his family were very kind to me. They always made me feel like part of the family. My friends reminded me often that I had it easier than other women my age."

Eiko smiled. "I am happy that you and Papa had two children. I love having Yu as my big brother. Speaking of Yu, did you see him this morning before he left for work? He was not feeling very well last night."

Etsuko looked surprised. "Oh? I did not know he was feeling ill. He was up before me. I heard his car engine warming up and then driving off. Maybe we should make him a nice supper."

Eiko nodded. "I could make curry rice, which is perfect on a cold day. It also keeps well, no matter how late he gets in from work."

Kiku entered the living room then and jumped onto the sofa. Meowing, she demanded their attention. Eiko was quick to acknowledge the cat's presence by scratching her ears and speaking softly to her, while Etsuko stroked the fur down Kiku's back.

She must be asking to go outside to walk in the fresh snow, Eiko thought. "I will let her out, Mother."

"I think it is too cold right now," Etsuko said. "Why not wait until later in the afternoon, when the sun might come out?"

Eiko nodded. "That is fine. Maybe I will go outside later with Kiku to enjoy the freshly fallen snow myself. I have missed it in Tokyo."

Eiko came downstairs, cheered to see a beautiful crackling fire in the fireplace. She found her mother in the kitchen, making two cups of *ocha* for them. "Let us take these to the living room so we can enjoy the fire," Etsuko suggested.

"Mom, that is sweet of you," Eiko said, turning to lead the way toward the fireplace. "Thank you for building the fire and making the ocha. I have missed having this special time with you since I moved away."

Once again, Eiko thought of how grateful she was that her parents had approved her plans to move to Tokyo after she graduated from university. *I know it was the right decision for me. I love the many unique places to visit in the Tokyo area and the mass transportation that works so efficiently to get the millions of residents and visitors to their destinations on time. But I also miss the unique beauty of my hometown.*

Eiko looked at her mother, who sat staring into the flames. "Mom, would you like to hear about my Christmas Eve day in Tokyo yesterday?"

Etsuko turned toward her daughter and smiled. "I have an hour before I need to leave for my *ikebana,* flower arrangement, class. It is just a short walk down the street and around the corner. Hiroshi's mother recently invited me to join the class as a guest. She did not want me to stay inside our house and do too much grieving for Papa."

Eiko saw her blink back her tears before she continued. "Today the class will be making a pair of *kadomatsu* decorations. I am looking forward to it, since the last few years I have purchased them at a store."

Eiko remembered the traditional New Year's god arrangement made of pine, bamboo, and plum tree branches, traditionally place outside the front door to welcome a certain Shinto god and provide a temporary home for it during the holidays. In return, they believed the god would bring happiness to each family on New Year's Day.

She did not answer my question, Eiko mused. *I wonder if she even heard me. Perhaps I should wait until another time to share my story with Mother. I do not want her to feel badly that I do not believe in Shinto gods any longer. Lord, what do I do? Please show me.*

"Go ahead, Eiko," Etsuko said. "Share what you wanted to share."

Eiko was relieved that her Mother had asked her to continue; she believed it was God's way of telling her to go ahead and share her story. She cleared her throat and began. "Actually, it started before Christmas Eve. I was at morning church on Sunday, December twentieth, and I felt Jesus touch my heart with His love and grace. I could not hold back any longer. I went up to the pastor and told him I believed in Jesus, that He is God's perfect Son, who came to earth to die for my wrongdoings. I told him I believed that Jesus was buried and rose again on the third day. To show the change in my heart, I was baptized at the Christmas Eve service last night, along with an older gentleman who also became a Christian that Sunday."

Eiko stopped talking, mindful to be sensitive to her Mother's reaction. Several moments went by without either of them speaking. Etsuko's eyes were locked on the ocha cup she held in her hands.

Dear Lord, what do I say now to help Mother understand? Eiko waited until she felt she knew which direction to go. "Mom, I know you are concerned for me because our family has always been Buddhist, but I just want you to know that Jesus Christ is a wonderful Friend and Savior. The Bible promises that He will always be with me and never leave me. He walks with me every day, in good times and bad. I am so happy to be a Christian—a Christ follower. Almighty God's gift to the world is His beloved Son. And God's Word, the Bible, teaches us how to live, love, and have peace and joy in our hearts."

Etsuko's expression was surprisingly serene as she responded. "This is really hard for me to take in, Eiko. I do not suppose it could be undone, could it? Truthfully, I wish you had never moved to Tokyo to live on your own. This would not have happened if you had stayed in Sapporo."

Tokyo is not the only place I could have heard about God's love, Eiko countered silently. *There are Christians everywhere. They are here in Sapporo. Surely, Mother has seen Christian churches around town. I feel sad that she blames my move for what she sees as a terrible outcome.*

"Maybe what I did sounds strange if I acted alone," she said, "but several friends who know me were at the church service on Christmas Eve when I was baptized. My friend Sayuri, who first shared God's love with me, as well as the church friends who were at the mountain retreat, were there to support me. Even Mr. Sakamoto from the fish market came, and Satoh, who asked me to his cousin's wedding in Yokohama. Also, I was told that my boss, Mr. Itoh, attended the service."

"That is nice, dear." Etsuko said without expression. "Maybe, if I had known, I would have been there, too."

Eiko laid a hand on her mother's forearm. "I knew you did not feel up to coming. It is all right, Mom. You can ask as many questions as you like, and I will do my best to answer each one. I want you to know everything there is to know. Do you have a question in mind now?"

The older woman shook her head. "No. I do not. I think I will put some more wood on the fire and then prepare my things for the class."

Eiko helped her mother with the logs, then excused herself and went upstairs to her bedroom. She sat down at her desk, deciding to work on her New Year's postcards, which she had purchased in Tokyo and brought with her. She had chosen several sets of cards, showing young ladies walking in a beautiful park in Tokyo, dressed in their festive New Year kimonos, with tall skyscrapers in the background. Eiko wrote a short comment on each postcard and then addressed them.

As she worked, she thought about what style of postcard she might want next year. When she was younger, she created her own cards, with special art supplies sold for that purpose. She knew that many people like to personalize their cards with a family photo, printed at a local print shop, with several templates to choose from. She thought that might be fun to do in the future.

She thought of other people she knew, who insisted on choosing postcards with the zodiac animals from the twelve-year cycle, which would be the dog in the coming year. In addition to New Year's postcards, many items would be sold in the shape of dogs or with dog designs printed on them. This had been part of Buddhist belief from ancient times, one in which each animal had a related patron deity.

Eiko loved the long-time tradition that required the post offices throughout Japan to hold all the New Year's postcards for special delivery on January first each year. The stack of postcards would have a rubber band placed around them to make the postman's job easier. How many relationships a person, or family, had with companies, coworkers, neighbors, acquaintances, and friends, determined how large the stack would be. Some people received only a few cards, while others received 100 or more.

The doorbell rang, interrupting Eiko's thoughts. She hurried downstairs and opened the front door. Her mother stood there, looking embarrassed and apologizing for leaving her house keys on the table.

"Come on in, Mom," Eiko said, standing back so she could open the door wide. "Can I help you with your decorations and bag?"

Her mother shook her head. "No, thanks. I am going to set one on each side of the door so they can be seen as people go by. You can take my bag of supplies, though."

Eiko brought the bag in and set it on the table beside the forgotten keys.

Etsuko came in and closed the door behind her. She hung up her coat and pulled off her snow boots. Eiko thought it appeared her mother had enjoyed a pleasant walk to the ikebana class in her neighborhood.

"Do you want some ocha, dear?" Etsuko asked.

"Yes, I would. Thank you." Eiko followed her mother into the kitchen so she could hear about the class.

❧ ❧ ❧

After the warm ocha and nice conversation, Eiko took Kiku out for a short romp. Then she finished her postcards and walked to the post office to mail them. When she got back, feeling exhilarated from her cold, brisk walk, she decided to start the curry rice for supper.

She cut up the vegetables and meat into bite-sized pieces and cooked them until tender on top of the stove. Then she put the measured rice into the rice cooker and set the timer. She finished up by making the sauce from dried curry blocks, water, and a little oil. Finally, she put the curry sauce, along with the vegetables and meat, into the same pan and let it all simmer. It wasn't long before the wonderful aroma of curry filled the downstairs area of the house.

As dinner simmered on the stove, the phone rang, and Eiko picked it up in the living room. "Moshi moshi."

"*Yu desu.* It is Yu. Eiko, I am sorry about last night. I was frustrated and took it out on you. That is why I want to be home early tonight to make it up to you. It is really nice to have you back home, even if you only get to stay for two weeks."

Eiko felt a few tears rise to the surface, threatening to overflow, but she squelched them. "I appreciate that, Yu," Eiko said humbly, blinking back the wetness.

"I am leaving my workplace now and coming home," Yu said. "What is for dinner?"

"Oh, how nice! It will be great to have you here to eat with us. I made beef curry." She could almost see the smile on Yu's face.

"That is perfect on a cold, wintry day. I will be there in forty minutes. Do not start without me."

Eiko beamed at the thought of the three of them spending the evening together. *I am sure You had something to do with Yu's decision, Lord. Thank You!*

When Yu got home from work, the three of them ate together at the kitchen table. After eating all they wanted, Eiko cleaned up. They watched some TV together and went to bed earlier than normal, each one expressing weariness. Kiku remained by the living room fireplace, seemingly unwilling to get up and follow her family upstairs until she was ready.

CHAPTER TWO

E iko awakened to the unique sounds of the city's snow-plow, working in front of her house. The back-up warning bell and the mechanical lift on the truck made constant noises as it got the job done to keep the streets clear. The only problem, after the snowplow moved on, would be a ridge across the entrance to every driveway, needing to be shoveled in order to get vehicles in or out.

Eiko got up and immediately changed into her snow pants and a warmer shirt. She put on her matching snow jacket, then opened her dresser drawer to grab a pair of wool socks. Lying next to her socks was a small, flat box that contained an expensive heart necklace that her friend Satoh had given her at Haneda airport in Tokyo the previous night. She had politely refused, uncomfortable at the extravagance and implied meaning of the gift, but Satoh insisted she take it. They were just friends at work but had gone out several times for lunch. Satoh told her how important she had become to him in the last few months. Thinking of that moment now, Eiko blushed, shut the drawer, and put her socks on.

Seeing the box also jogged Eiko's memory about a package her mother had said would be in her room when she got back to Sapporo. Her uncle's best friend had something to give Eiko that had belonged to her papa. He had dropped the package off earlier in the month, and Eiko's mother had told her on the phone that she left the package in her room. *I do not see it anywhere. I need to ask Mother where it is. I am anxious to see what is in it.*

Eiko walked down the stairs, stepped outside to the carport, and scanned the area for her favorite aluminum snow shovel. She found it and went straight to work.

Sometime later, happy to see she was making good progress, Eiko decided to take a five-minute break. Standing still for a moment, while resting on her shovel, she noticed the other women on her street working on the same task, in order to make sure the men in their houses could leave for work without any delays.

Twenty more minutes of concentrated effort was all it took, and Eiko was done. She removed her boots in the carport and went into the house, where she took off her jacket and hung it on a peg, just inside the kitchen door. Then she went into the living room to put another log on the fire, before returning to the kitchen to make a quick breakfast of toast and coffee.

Mother joined her almost immediately, smiling a little as she teased her daughter. "By the way, how was it shoveling snow?"

"It was actually fun," Eiko admitted, "but my muscles are feeling it now. It will be wonderful to get into the *ofuro* for a good soak tonight after dinner. I am sure I will sleep well."

Etsuko nodded. "Yes, I believe so."

"So, Mom," she said, taking another sip of coffee, "can I fix you something to eat? I am just having toast, but I would be happy to cook you something else."

Etsuko waved away the offer. "No, thank you, Eiko. I already had a little something earlier, and I am not hungry right now."

Eiko set her cup on the table as a thought popped into her mind. "By the way, Mom, do you remember the package you placed in my room several weeks ago after Uncle's best friend dropped by? It was something that belonged to Papa that he wanted me to have."

Etsuko lifted her eyebrows. "Oh, that package. I left it in your room, but Kiku got hold of it and tore up the wrapping. I took it out of your room, meaning to replace the wrapping before you came, but now I am not sure where I put it. I will search for it another time. It is around here somewhere."

Eiko tried not to let the disappointment show on her face, as she did not want to upset her mother. She decided to wait a day or two and then ask again. Missing her beloved papa so much, Eiko could not wait to have something of his in her hands to treasure through the years.

As Mother excused herself to go upstairs, Eiko heard her greet Yu with a friendly "ohayou gozaimasu," as they passed one another on the stairs. Eiko was pleased that her brother was coming down to join her. Having anticipated his coming, she had prepared some yogurt and fresh fruit for him. As soon as he was seated at the table, she placed it in front of him, along with some toast and coffee.

"Arigatou," Yu said. "Not only for the breakfast but also for shoveling the driveway so I can go to work." His face appeared sad. "I am sorry that I must go in today, on a Saturday, to help my team finish our work project, even though my responsibilities are already finished. I had hoped to spend more time with you while you are here."

Eiko looked at her big brother, dressed in a suit and tie and looking all grown up. "I am sorry, too. I know things have not been easy for you, Yuitsu, since Papa died. You and Papa always got along so well because of your similarities. I know that being there for Mother has been difficult. I want to help as much as I can, so let us stay close and be strong for each other, okay?"

Yu got a pained look on his face but nodded. He ran his hand through his black hair, which made it stand up. "I have some bad habits now, Eiko. I guess I am not the brother you thought you were coming home to greet."

Eiko's heart twisted. "Yu, what do you mean? What is going on?"

He shrugged. "In a way...I have become dependent on alcohol to help me function at work and at home. I am just too stressed all the time. Actually, I thought about going drinking with my coworkers yesterday, but they were all busy." He offered a weak smile. "I am glad I came home instead."

Eiko felt knots forming in her stomach. *What am I supposed to say? One thing for sure: I need to show God's grace to Yu.* "Thank you for being truthful. It is a wonderful character trait, one that I love. I could always go to you for the truth when we were growing up." Eiko got up and stepped toward him so she could lean down and hug him.

"Did you know that Creator God loves you, even though you have messed up? We have all messed up, doing things that harm us. That is why God sent His perfect Son, Jesus Christ, to earth. He took upon His body all of our wrongdoings and died on the Cross to take our punishment. That amazing love is called grace, and we did not do anything to deserve it. He pardons us and sets us free when we ask with hearts of faith."

With no more than a nod to affirm that he'd heard his sister's words, Yu finished his toast and drank a few more sips of coffee, as Eiko returned to her seat. She could only hope he would consider her words as the day progressed.

Kiku came into the kitchen then, no doubt to be sure she was not missing something. She rubbed against Yu's legs, then walked over to Eiko and did the same. She meowed several times, demanding to be petted. Eiko smiled. Kiku always expected someone to pay attention to her right away.

Still stroking Kiku, Eiko turned her attention back to Yu.

His shoulders dropped as he made a confession. "My drinking was going on even before you left for Tokyo."

Eiko was surprised. "I am sorry, Yu. I did not know you were hurting. I was too much into myself to see your pain, I guess."

He lifted his head and looked her in the eye. "That is okay, Eiko. I tried to hide my troubles from everyone, but people at work started noticing when I was not at my best in the mornings."

"Is it your job?"

He took a deep breath. "Somewhat, yes. I feel bored at work. I am not progressing in my career as fast as I had hoped. I have been working for this company for five years, since I graduated from college. I have no personal life at all; work has completely taken over my time. I need a purpose for my life, Eiko, but I do not know how to find one."

Kiku meowed again, and this time Eiko picked her up and placed her on her lap. "I do not know how to fix your heart's longings, Yu, but Jesus does. And He will, if you ask Him."

Yu shook his head dejectedly. "I would not know what to say, Eiko. I do not know Him, as you seem to."

Breathing a silent prayer for God's help, Eiko said, "It is not hard. In fact, it is easy. Just say, 'God, I need your help. Please show me what I should do.' "

"I will think about it, Eiko. Right now I need to leave." Yu stood up, but with a slightly softer expression on his face than when he'd come in. He left the room, no doubt to get his jacket and briefcase.

I am so worried about him, Lord. Please help him trust in You for the help he needs.

Eiko carried Kiku into the living room and gently placed her on Etsuko's lap.

"Oh, there you are, Kiku. Where have you been?" Etsuko's eyes had been closed when Eiko walked in, but she opened them as soon as she felt the cat on her lap. She looked up at Eiko. "I heard you and your brother talking. I think he has missed you."

Eiko shrugged. "I do not know about that, but I know I have missed him."

Both of them left the living room and went to tell Yu goodbye, as he headed out to the carport.

The ladies closed the door after him and went back into the living room, where they sat down in front of the fire and began to plan their day.

"You have not had much breakfast, Mom. Would you like something before I clean up the kitchen?"

Etsuko shook her head. "What I had earlier was enough. To be truthful, I am still full from the curry rice last night. I ate two helpings, which is more than I usually eat." She smiled. "I enjoyed having company for dinner."

"I am glad I could be here." Eiko watched Kiku, sitting contentedly on Etsuko's lap. "I am sorry, Mom, that you have been so lonely since Papa died. Being single and on my own, I know what it feels like to eat alone. Sometimes it is fine, and then other days, I would love to have someone to share a meal with."

Etsuko sighed deeply. "Yu has not been home lately. He stays out late. When he comes home, he is not interested in eating a meal. I think he probably eats before he gets here."

Eiko smiled, hoping to encourage her mother. "Well, last night was super special. All three of us ate together.

While I am here for the holidays and beyond, I hope we will make some happy memories around our kitchen table again. That is one of my prayers that I am asking Jesus for."

Eiko reached for her Bible on the low coffee table in front of the sofa. She opened it to the book of Luke and reread the story of Jesus Christ's birth, thinking about the holiday that Christians celebrate each year on December 25th. *It is when Immanuel, "God-with-us," came to earth to live among us.*

She sighed contentedly. *Jesus, according to God's good plan, forever changed the direction of our lives and the course of world history.* Eiko never ceased to be amazed at the enormity of such a thought.

She finished reading and began to pray softly. "Lord Jesus, thank You for Your love for me and my family. I trust in Your good plan for us. Thank You that I could share Your good news with my family. It was a wonderful way to celebrate Your birthday, Jesus. I love You. Amen."

As Eiko got up from the sofa and turned up the heater, Kiku came running, no doubt anxious to be a part of whatever Eiko was up to. Eiko was pleased to see, out the double-paned picture window in the living room, that the snowstorm was over, and the sun was peering through the morning clouds. It seemed chilly in the house, so she knew the outside temperature must still be quite low.

Eiko thought about what she wanted to do for the day, deciding to call Sayuri in Tokyo to see how she was doing.

"Moshi moshi," she heard when she placed the call. "This is Sayuri."

"Good morning, Sayuri. This is Eiko, calling from Sapporo. How are you?"

Eiko could almost see the smile on her friend's face. "I am enjoying my Saturday away from work. I have been reading an interesting book by a famous Japanese author, who is a Christian. I look forward to actually finishing this one because next week we get our five days off for the New Year holidays." She paused for a moment, then asked, "How about you, Eiko? Is everything going okay with you?"

"It feels good to be home with my family," Eiko admitted, "but we have all changed since Papa's funeral. It seems we are learning how to relate to each other again." She caught herself as a thought flickered through her mind. "I am really sorry, Sayuri. I have not even asked you if you are going to be with your family during the New Year celebration."

"Yes, I am. I have not been back to my hometown in three years. After praying about it, I thought it was the right thing to do. I am going there on January second, and I will return to Tokyo on the fourth."

"I hope the time with your family will go wonderfully," Eiko said, meaning every word she spoke. "God is teaching us both how important it is to be with family. That is why I asked Mr. Itoh, our boss, if he would allow me stay for another week after the holiday time is over. My mother and brother need some tender loving care."

They talked for a few more minutes before hanging up, having promised to write letters with more details. The two work friends had grown close since Sayuri introduced Eiko to Jesus Christ and encouraged her to be part of her church family.

Eiko's thoughts then turned to Satoh, her other friend from work, who had expressed his interest in having a deeper relationship with her. Eiko was touched by his gift to her at Christmas, but she did not want to rush into anything, so she had asked Satoh for more time to think it over.

She definitely knew she had feelings for him as a friend, and for the most part, enjoyed being with him. Every once in a while, though, when Satoh got moody and walked away, she became uncomfortable. She wished he would not do that.

I wonder if he is expecting me to call. I have only been gone for two days. I think it might be too soon. I will wait a few more days and then call and wish him Happy New Year, akemashite omedetou gozaimasu, *on New Year's Day!*

She went into the kitchen and got the rice ready for the rice cooker. She also took out the *shake,* or salmon, and cooked it in a pan. After the rice was done, she formed it to her hand and put some flaked salmon in the middle before she made sure it was covered up by the rice, as it was pressed together in a triangular shape. She then picked up a piece of the cut *nori,* seaweed, to wrap around the triangle, and one *onigiri* was done. Eiko knew hers were not as delicious as her mom's or Mrs. Sakamoto's back in Tokyo. *It will take years to earn that reputation. The older women have done it so many times, they do not think about what they are doing because their hands are so well practiced.*

Eiko heard her mother's approaching footsteps. "Are you ready for some lunch?" Eiko called out. "I made salmon *onigiri* for us."

"Sure, dear. That would be nice."

Etsuko sat down at the kitchen table and asked her daughter for some ocha. Eiko had it ready and poured her mother a cup. Then she got out two little black lacquer trays for the onigiri.

"Here you go, Mom. Would it be okay if I said a prayer before we eat?"

Etsuko shrugged. "It does not bother me. Go ahead."

Eiko sat across from her mother. "God, we thank you for your provision at meal time and for your love throughout our day and night. Please bring health to our bodies and joy to our souls. In Jesus' name, I pray. Amen."

Mother took a bite and smiled. "Eiko, I think this is your best onigiri ever."

"I am sure it is because Hokkaido's salmon is so tasty. I am glad you like it. I made several if you would like another one."

While the two of them enjoyed their light lunch, Mother asked Eiko if she would like to watch the all-Japan ice-skating championship, which was scheduled to start in a few minutes. Eiko agreed, and they moved to the living room and turned on the TV. Eiko was happy to watch it with her mother. Several of the Japanese skaters were also medal contenders in the international competitions. The event took place in the ice arena in Tokyo. The exciting program included the ladies' and men's sections, and they went on all afternoon.

Kiku had fallen asleep on Eiko's lap during the program, but now she was awake and seemed to want to play. The cat jumped down and appeared to be searching for something. *Her mouse toy, no doubt*, Eiko thought. Eiko got down on the floor to help Kiku look, and sure enough, she found it in a stack of wood, sitting on the hearth near the fireplace. After tossing it around and getting Kiku to retrieve it, Eiko soon noticed the cat seemed bored and had quit playing.

"Mom, I was thinking that for dinner tonight we could order from the local restaurant that delivers," Eiko said, leaving Kiku's toy on the floor, as she turned her attention to her mother. "Does that sound good to you? Some noodles, like *udon* or *soba*, would taste good. What do you think? We could do it when Yu gets home. It does not take very long for them to send it out with a driver on a small motorized scooter."

Etsuko nodded, seemingly pleased at the suggestion. "Yes. That would be fine."

With the cat curled up next to the fireplace and sleeping again, Eiko and her mother spent time reading, as they waited for Yu to come home. He did not arrive quite as early as the previous night, nor did he call first, but overall he came through for Eiko and Mother. They all enjoyed their meal choices, which were delivered quickly and conveniently. When they finished, they set the dishes out on the porch for the driver to pick up later. Then they went into the living room, where Yu built a lovely fire for them all to enjoy.

As they sat there, gazing into the flames, Mother reminded them that Grandma and Uncle Kenta were coming on Tuesday to spend the New Year holidays with them.

"How about if we all go to an *onsen*, a natural hot springs?" Yu suggested. "You know, for an overnight trip together." The look on his face was expectant, as he waited for their response.

"Oh, that would be fun—and relaxing," Eiko declared, catching Yu's enthusiasm immediately.

Etsuko's response was a bit slower and more measured. "We have not done that in a long time," she admitted. "But the reservations are all booked up, I imagine."

"I will call tomorrow and check on it—if it has your approval, Mother," Yu offered, his joy at their response evident on his face.

"That does sound like a good idea," Mother agreed. "Why not try?"

A lightness seemed to develop in the room, as Eiko thought about how much fun it would be to go and do something special with Grandma and their uncle. She imagined the others were thinking similar thoughts. *Papa's mother*

*and oldest brother have been on other trips together with our fam-
ily... while Papa was still alive.*

The fire crackled and popped loudly then, and Kiku
jumped up and sideways, away from the hearth.

Etsuko chuckled. "We will need to ask a neighbor to
come and check on Kiku. Too bad she cannot participate,
since she is an important member of the family."

Eiko smiled and then changed the subject. "Yu, I would
also love to go skiing with you one time during the holidays.
Are you interested? We can see who is faster these days.
Who knows? You might have gotten slower since you aged."
Eiko let out a giggle, knowing Yuitsu was an excellent skier
and had not changed a bit.

He grinned. "Sure. I am up to your challenge. I get
three days off from work. Why not call one or two of the
local ski resorts and see what their schedules are for January
first to third?"

"I will," she promised. "And I will let you know."

After a pleasant day, and with a nice family trip planned,
all three of them took their turn soaking in the ofuro and
then went on to have a great, stress-free night of sleep.

CHAPTER THREE

On Sunday morning, everyone was up early to eat Mother's breakfast of fish, rice, and *miso* soup, made of fermented soybean paste. Today's soup had small squares of tofu in the broth. Everyone ate to their heart's content, and then cleaned up together.

Eiko announced that since it was Sunday, she wanted to go check out the church that her friend Hope was a part of when she volunteered for two years in Sapporo. Eiko asked if anyone would like to go with her.

"I thought your friend was back in America now," Etsuko said, appearing confused.

"She is, Mom," Eiko explained. "But her church still has a worship service every Sunday. She gave me the address and phone number before she left. I thought it would be nice to see what her church is like. Hope said there are a lot of young career folks attending, as well as college kids. Yu, it would be people our age. Do you want to go with me?"

"Maybe some other time. I promised my friend I would play some indoor basketball with him at the gym today. With my social life nearly nonexistent, I do not want to miss this."

Eiko nodded, remembering their earlier conversation. "I understand, Yu. Mom, do you have plans?"

"Actually, my friend asked if she could visit me this morning to see how I am doing. That is why I got up so early.

I am looking forward to her visit. She has been a friend for forty-six years, since we were in elementary school. You both know Keiko san. She lives in Chitose now, so I do not get to see her very often. But she still drives and visits Sapporo when she can."

"I remember her giving us our first ski equipment when we were kids," Eiko said. "Her children had grown and could not use them anymore."

"It was quality stuff," Yu added.

Mother filled in the rest of the story. "Keiko's husband had been an Olympic ski jumper before she met him. Do you remember? Several years later, he had a financial arrangement with a ski-goods store to carry his image and name in some of their product lines. So the skis he purchased for his family were all at cost. Their kids had the best skis of anybody on the slope."

Yu laughed. "Maybe that is why we learned to ski so easily."

"It is more likely that you are both great skiers because your Father took you almost every Sunday," Etsuko said with a wistful smile. "He loved to ski with you. I remember when he came home and told me he was so proud of you both for skiing a difficult diamond run."

Eiko nodded. "I remember that. My heart was racing as fast as my skis."

Yu then reminded them of how frozen the trees were at the top of the mountain the day he skied down the trail reserved for experts. Each time he exhaled, he could see his breath move through the cold air.

They found the times with their father were fun to discuss, so they continued to reminisce. It was an enjoyable time, but after that conversation, they went their separate ways for the rest of the day.

❧ ❧ ❧

Eiko caught the bus that went to the main bus station downtown, where she then caught another bus to the church. In about thirty minutes, she was there. *This building does not look like a church. It looks more like a retail store. Even the sign resembles one that would be on a business. But it has the church's name on it, and it looks rather inviting to newcomers.* Upon entering, Eiko noticed large, colorful, scripture art-deco wall-hangings. Several young adults stood around to greet people as they entered.

Once inside, Eiko saw a young man with slacks and a casual shirt, walking toward her with a big smile. "Good morning. Welcome to our church. Is this your first time to visit us?"

She nodded. "Yes, it is."

"How did you hear about us?"

Eiko smiled, as she thought of her friend, whom she met at the hospital in Sapporo when Eiko's papa was in a coma and not expected to live. "I learned about your church from Hope Tanner."

A smile lit the young man's face. "Oh, great! We all miss Hope now that she has returned to America. My name is Hideki. What is yours?"

"I am Eiko. I live in Tokyo now, but I came back to my *furusato*, hometown, for the New Year holidays."

"It is nice to have you with us today, Eiko san."

"Arigatou. Thank you."

Eiko headed toward the large seating area and sat down. She looked around and noticed about 100 folding chairs, set in rows, and a stage at the front, with band equipment, including guitars, drum set, keyboard, and five mic stands. The stage included some props that looked like they might be part of the pastor's message. The two props were six-foot by five-foot "books." One had the title "Psalms" and the other "Proverbs," written on their spines.

The band came out on the stage to do a sound check, as the people continued to come in. Eiko noticed a young lady on stage, who was playing the electric base. The type of music they played was louder than at her church in Tokyo. At her church, the music was folksier, with a pianist and two acoustic guitar players.

Eiko looked around at the gathering crowd once again. This time she saw that the room was comfortably full, with mostly young people between their upper teens to twenty-somethings.

Eiko's church had a group of about twenty college and career adults, and the group had special meaning to her. They were the ones who befriended her at the mountain retreat and encouraged her in her faith-journey with Jesus Christ. Even now, she knew they were praying for her while she was away from Tokyo. And she prayed for them, especially for Sayuri, as she returned to her hometown to visit her family she hadn't seen in three years.

The worship service started with prayer and then a half-hour of praise music, led by the band. There were five singers—three young men and two young ladies. They, along with the instrumentalists, were all gifted in music and produced a nice, smooth sound together. Some people in the crowd lifted their hands in worship, as the message in the lyrics touched their hearts. Eiko closed her eyes as she sang with the crowd the familiar song she had learned at the mountain retreat. As she did so, her heart overflowed with God's love for her. When the praise time ended, she opened her eyes and saw the pastor come up on stage to begin his message.

"How many of you love the idea of searching for treasure?" he asked. "Okay. I can see a lot of you raising your hands. Good. How many of you have actually found treasure?" All but two people dropped their hands. The pastor nodded and smiled. "Go ahead and tell me what you found. How about you?" He pointed to the woman on the left side of the room.

She responded in a loud voice so everyone could hear. "A 5,000-yen bill on the street."

Then the pastor asked the man who had kept his hand raised. "How about you? What treasure did you find?"

He quickly answered, "A keyboard in good condition at 'big trash' day in the neighborhood."

The pastor continued his inquiry of the two. "Have you found any treasures since then?" Both responded that they had not.

"Treasures on earth are not easy to come by, are they?" he continued. "But heavenly treasures from God are plenti-ful...if we search for them. God's Word, the Bible, is a rich treasure book." The pastor pointed to the two props on the stage. "Today we are going to talk about two of the sixty-six books in the Bible. Help me out. Which ones?"

The crowd answered in unison, "Psalms and Proverbs."

The pastor went on. "Psalms is a treasure book of poems, written by several men, who were inspired by Almighty God to write them. The poems were often set to music, becom-ing hymns that were then used as prayers in worship. When reading the Psalms, we can often see our own thoughts and feelings expressed beautifully and passionately to God. Many of the psalms end with words of praise to God for His love, faithfulness, saving power, guidance, and mercy. These character traits remind us of how awesome God really is."

Eiko liked the pastor's message. She continued to lis-ten as he read several passages from Psalms and told them that it is the longest book in the Bible, having 150 chapters. He also taught them that if they opened the Bible to the middle, they would find Psalms quickly.

I definitely would like to read the Psalms, Eiko thought, *but I will need to buy a complete Bible, one that has the Old Testament as well as the New. My Bible, which I got as a gift at my employer's wife's wake, is only the New Testament. It begins with the birth of Jesus Christ. I have come to understand that the Old Testament is everything that happened before that, starting with God's creation. I really need the whole Bible now, since I became a follower of Jesus Christ and was baptized.*

Eiko had been lost in her thoughts for a moment. Now she listened as the pastor moved on to the book of Proverbs, which he explained follows the book of Psalms.

"Proverbs," the pastor said, "contains short sayings about wisdom for daily living. So many of the questions people have about God's ways can be answered in Proverbs."

The pastor then read and discussed several passages in Proverbs. Afterward he had a challenge for the group. "Who will commit to read something from Psalms and Proverbs every day this week?" About half said they would do it. Eiko thought she should not lift her hand, since she needed to purchase a complete Bible first.

The pastor then prayed for everyone and dismissed them. Eiko walked slowly through the crowd until she reached the front door. Outside, a young lady with a gray winter jacket walked up to her. "Hi! I am Mari. I was at the hospital with Hope the day you were there visiting your father. We sat next to you in the hospital cafeteria that day. Do you remember? Hope recently told me that your father passed away. I am sad for you, but I am praying that you will experience God's peace in your heart."

Eiko nodded. Yes, she did remember meeting this quiet young woman. "Thank you, Mari san. It is so kind of you to remember me. How did you spot me in the crowd?"

"I was one of the five praise singers. I looked out at the congregation and spotted you when we were singing the third worship song. I think God helped by pointing you out to me. How long will you be in Sapporo?"

"About ten more days. I wanted to visit Hope's church while I was in town. I really enjoyed it. If I lived here, I think I would choose to join this church. But I also love my church in Tokyo. They have become like family to me. I praise God for them."

Mari took a piece of paper and pen out of her black leather purse. "Eiko san, may I please have your telephone number? I would like to take you out for a donut before you return to Tokyo. May I call you after the holidays?"

Eiko smiled and took the pen. "That would be fun, Mari san. Thank you for asking." They said their goodbyes, then Eiko walked to the nearby bus stop, just as the large city bus pulled up. Eiko paid her fare and found a seat. *I was so blessed by being at church. After today, I am excited to start reading Psalms and Proverbs. But I really need to get a new Bible right away.* After the bus driver pulled in to the big downtown station, Eiko got off to change to her neighborhood bus line.

Eiko hoped to see both Yu and Mother at home when she got back. "Hi, Mom," Eiko said as she entered the living room and spotted her mother on the sofa. "How was your time with your longtime friend?" She looked around. "And where is Yu? Still out with his friend?"

Etsuko looked up from her usual spot in front of the fireplace, though no flames crackled or warmed the room. Kiku rested on Etsuko's lap. Etsuko beamed a smile at her daughter, warming Eiko's heart to see her mother smile.

"Yes, I believe he is. And my time with my friend was good. We talked about old times. What about you?"

"I had a great time at Hope's church. Everyone was friendly and kind. One of Hope's friends, Mari, asked me to meet her for donuts after the holidays."

Etsuko smiled. "That is nice, dear. But do not forget that you have friends from high school, who are hoping to see you while you are here. You should give them a call and try to meet up with some of them after the holidays."

Eiko nodded. "Yes, you are right. I should probably do that. Right now, though, I want to call my friend Satoh in Tokyo to see how he is doing. Would you like for me to build you a fire first?"

"Yes, thank you. That would be nice. Before Yu left this morning, he brought in some more wood, so there should be plenty."

Eiko finished her task and then went to her room to call Satoh. They had a nice conversation, catching up with each other. Satoh was curious about her church experience and thought it sounded really different than the churches he had visited with Eiko for their employer's wife's wake, his cousin Aki's wedding, and the children's Christmas party they helped put on. With the promise from Satoh that he would call on New Year's Day, they concluded their phone conversation.

Eiko heard Kiku making a familiar noise. *Probably trying to play with her mouse toy*, Eiko thought, so she went off to find her and join in her game. Eiko thought the exercise might help Kiku, her loyal feline, sleep better tonight and not stay up.

Later, Eiko suggested to her mother that they go out together and get their hair cut. "I know my shoulder-length hair could use a trim, and you could get yours set in your favorite style. It would be nice to get it done before Grandma and Uncle Kenta arrive in two more days. What do you think?"

Etsuko nodded. "Perhaps that would feel nice. I have not been to the hair salon in the month and a half since your father passed away."

"Perfect. I will be there with you, so you do not have to be alone."

Eiko went to the hall closet and got out their warm coats. After a few moments, they were on their way in a taxi. The owners of the small hair salon welcomed Etsuko and her daughter as they entered. It was not very busy, so Mother got right in. Eiko waited about twenty minutes before she got called to the stylist's chair. While getting her cut, she was asked about her new life in Tokyo. Eiko happily shared a few stories about big-city life.

Eiko then noticed that Mother was quiet when her stylist asked how she was doing these days, expressing how much they'd missed seeing her. It was obvious the store owners had been concerned about Etsuko's absence, but they seemed to understand that she had lost her husband and was still grieving.

Eiko and Mother returned home in the late afternoon, hoping to see that Yu had come home after his day of basketball with his friend. But the house was empty when they arrived. They ate dinner alone, just the two of them—and Kiku, of course—but without Yu. "I guess he is having too much fun to return home yet," Mother commented, in what sounded like a hopeful tone.

"Since he had to work yesterday, maybe he is trying to make the most of his free time today," Eiko suggested. "You know, stretching it to make it last."

"Well, Yu being home the last two nights in a row for dinner is a miracle." Etsuko smiled, but her expression was touched with sadness. "I did not really expect it to last."

Eiko decided it was time to change the subject. "Mom, let us watch a little TV or read for a while. He might come home by then."

"Yes. That sound like a good idea. That funny quiz show is on tonight. Maybe laughter will help brighten my mood."

There was indeed plenty of laughter throughout the program, and Eiko could tell that it did seem to bolster Etsuko's spirits, despite the fact that Yu still had not come in. When the quiz show ended, they decided to watch a detective program, with a famous Japanese celebrity. When that was over, Mother turned off the TV. "Well, I am going to go take an ofuro and get in bed. Goodnight, Eiko."

"Goodnight, Mom. I am going to stay up another hour or so, to catch up on some reading."

Eiko dozed off several times while reading, and each time she did so, Kiku came and licked her face. Eiko decided she might as well take an ofuro and go to bed. She left two lights on for her brother, and Kiku followed right behind her as she left the room.

CHAPTER FOUR

The next morning Eiko got out of bed early, hoping to have a chance to talk with Yu before he left for work. She went downstairs to a dark kitchen, surprised he wasn't there.

Eiko turned on the light, turned up the central heater, and began to make coffee. She also made some soft-boiled eggs and a leafy salad. Yu came in as Eiko was putting it all out on the table. She completed the setting with two plates and their personal chopsticks. Then she poured two coffees and sat down across from Yu.

"Good morning, Brother. How are you this morning?"

Yu yawned before answering. "Very tired."

"So I see. You stayed out late last night. Were you drinking?"

He ducked his eyes. "I might have had a few. Are you counting, Sister?"

"You said you only drink when you are stressed out. Did you not have a stress-free Sunday with a friend, doing something you enjoy? Where's the stress in that?"

When Yu didn't answer, Eiko said a short prayer, thanking God for the food, and then started on her eggs and salad. Yu appeared to be concentrating on his own breakfast and, therefore, not open to more discussion.

Eiko got up to serve more coffee, pleased that her brother seemed to be enjoying the breakfast she had prepared. Just as they were finishing up, Etsuko came down to join them.

Eiko smiled and greeted her mother, then asked, "Mom, would you like some breakfast this morning?"

Etsuko returned the smile. "Yes, please." Before long, she, too was enjoying the breakfast Eiko had prepared.

As soon as he'd cleaned his plate, Yu gathered his coat and briefcase, obviously preparing to leave for work.

"Today is the last day of work before your holidays begin," Eiko said, hoping to encourage him. "I'm praying for you today, Yu."

Before he could respond, she got up and gave him a hug. "I cannot wait to see you again tonight after work. Maybe we can watch a TV movie together."

Yu's glasses and smile reminded her of her papa. "Maybe we can," he said. "See you tonight."

"Do not forget that Grandma and Uncle Kenta will be coming tomorrow to join us for the holidays," Etsuko called after him.

Yu's "okay" could be heard faintly as he went out the door to the carport.

"Mom," Eiko said, once Yu was gone, "what do you need me to do to get ready for Papa's family?"

Etsuko looked thoughtful. "They will be staying in the *tatami* room, since it is spacious enough for two. Besides, I know they enjoy sleeping on the traditional flooring made from rice straw mats. The clean futons and covers are in the futon closet, which you can set out right before they arrive. If you do not mind, the room also needs dusting before they come."

"Sure, Mom. I will be glad to do that." Eiko knew the tatami room was a special room in the house. It especially reminded her mother of the old days, when Japanese rooms were all tatami. That is where their Buddhist family altar was located, as well as a special display area for a beautiful wall hanging, written in Japanese calligraphy and penned by a brush. Other items of beauty and worth, such as antiques, were also kept in the tatami room.

Eiko's apartment in Tokyo did not come with such a traditional room, but their family home had its tatami room right off the living room area. Eiko loved the sliding doors, which made a special sound as they rolled on their track. Eiko was pleased that their guests would use that room.

"Everything should be nice," Eiko commented. "I am glad it worked out for all of us to go to the onsen while they are here. It will be perfect! We will spend the night at the hot springs lodge, and then come back on New Year's Eve. We can have our traditional soba on the way home. I love buckwheat noodles!"

She paused for a moment. "I think Uncle Kenta will want to go to the Buddhist temple after we get back, for the ringing of the bells, which ends at midnight. Afterward he will certainly buy a blessing and come home, don't you think?"

Etsuko was still eating, so she nodded her head in agreement.

"Mother, I do not want to go to the temple this year and worship like I did all the years before," Eiko ventured, butterflies flitting around in her stomach. She pushed on. "My Savior, Jesus Christ, suffered and died for me on the Cross, so that I could be forgiven and live in a right relationship with Creator God. He has done so much for me. I want to worship Him only."

Etsuko swallowed her food, then sighed. "I do not have the strength to fight you, Eiko. Do as you wish. But you might get some criticism from Uncle Kenta and Grandmother. You will have to handle that by yourself. I am not going to defend your attitude or actions. You are on your own."

Relief washed over Eiko, quieting her accelerated heart-beat. "I understand, Mother. Thank you."

Papa's family arrived safely, and Eiko was so pleased to have them there. Grandma had made some of the special foods at her home and brought them with her. They were traditional New Year's dishes, known as *osechi ryouri*, served in special lacquer compartmentalized boxes, which can be stacked, one on top of the other. Eiko knew that each dish had a special meaning for celebrating the New Year. An added bonus was that the foods could be made a few days ahead, enabling women to relax and enjoy the family times together, rather than spending all day in the kitchen, while others celebrated.

Eiko smiled as she watched her grandmother. The woman was eighty-five years old and going strong. She insisted on being in the kitchen to prepare for every meal. Occasionally, Mother walked in to help her. Eiko, on the other hand, removed herself from the kitchen while Grandma was there. The woman was amazing! Everyone enjoyed her food, as it was so authentic and tasty.

The next day, everyone packed up and departed for the onsen, up in the mountains, about two hours away. They took two cars because there were too many to ride comfortably in one. Yu and Eiko rode in the white Nissan, while Mother and Grandmother rode with Uncle Kenta in his car. Kiku had obviously enjoyed the extra company and attention, but Eiko thought she seemed sad as everyone left her behind, to be checked on by a neighborhood friend.

The snowy scenery on the ride to the onsen was breathtaking, so much so that they were surprised when they realized they had arrived. They pulled into the parking area around four-thirty in the afternoon, close to dusk. Once inside the entryway, they removed their shoes and placed them on shelves, with other guests' shoes. Grandmother was the first to slide her feet into the inn's guest slippers, so Etsuko decided to tease her. "You are sure in a hurry to get in the hot springs," she said with a grin.

Grandma nodded. "It has been a while, dear, since I have had the pleasure of relaxing in an onsen. The natural healing mineral water sure helps an old woman's aches go away."

After checking in at the counter with their luggage, they were led to two side-by-side tatami rooms on the second floor. Grandmother, Mother, and Eiko were in one room, and the two men, Yu and Uncle Kenta, were in the other. Eiko immediately felt at home in the vintage Japanese inn, with wooden floors that creaked as guests walked on them, and she was certain the others felt the same way. She had heard that the old innkeeper occasionally shared stories of famous individuals who had stayed there in the past. She doubted they would be there long enough to hear one of his stories this time.

Before going to their rooms, the family decided to meet at the onsen entrance, which was down the hallway, in thirty minutes. The second-floor entrance allowed the guests to reach the attached onsen building, without having to be outside in the weather. As expected, Grandma was the first to arrive at their meeting place, with Uncle Kenta and Yu being the last to show up. When they entered the second floor of the onsen, they noticed coin-operated massage chairs, drink-vending machines, and two large-screen TV's, with benches all around. The lounging area was perfect for relaxing before or after using the onsen.

They climbed a wide staircase, which led to the first level, where they found a check-in counter and a place to buy tickets. With tickets in hand, guys went one way to their secure area, and women to the other.

Once inside the women's area, Eiko, her mother, and her grandmother looked for their assigned lockers, which matched the key bracelet they had received at the desk. Leaving their personal items in the lockers, they headed into the washing area, carrying their customary onsen white towel. An abundance of small plastic stools sat stacked up, next to plastic buckets. Next, they spotted equally spaced faucets, near the floor, with long covered drains. About two feet above each of the low faucets they saw removable shower heads to use if preferred.

Eiko grabbed the removable shower head and sat down on the small plastic stool. Etsuko did the same. Grandmother, however, decided to bathe the old-fashioned way. After getting the faucet water to the temperature she wanted, she grabbed a plastic, bowl-shaped bucket, filled it, and poured it over her head and body. As she soaped up, the bucket was placed where it could fill up with more water.

Eiko was amazed at her grandmother's agility and patience. "Grandmother, are you all right?" she inquired. "Do you need any help getting up from your stool?"

The older woman shook her head. "I have got it. Go ahead and get in the onsen. I will join you in a moment."

Eiko and Etsuko walked over to one of several large soaking pools and checked several things before climbing in. The main thing they wanted to know was the water temperature, but they also read a posted notice that detailed what natural minerals from the hot springs were in that particular pool, and what the health benefits were from that combination of minerals. How long anyone stayed in the pools was a personal choice. Eiko saw that some older women folded up their towels and laid them on top of their heads, while they enjoyed the rejuvenating mineral hot springs. Other ladies sat in silence, and some, who were there with companions, engaged in an occasional conversation.

Eiko chose a different pool than her mother and grandmother, one that offered a higher temperature than theirs. She eased herself in, slowly adjusting to the temperature.

Eiko looked at her grandmother and mother. The older woman saw her watching them and smiled in obvious contentment. "This is heavenly," she murmured.

Etsuko nodded. "But remember," she cautioned. "You have to get out before you get over-heated."

After Eiko, Grandma, and Etsuko were finished, they all got out, rinsed off again at the bathing area, and returned to the dressing area, where they availed themselves of hair dryers and a few amenities, like lotions and cotton swabs. As soon as they were dressed, they left their locker keys at the desk, then waited for Yu and Uncle Kenta to join them.

While they waited, the ladies went upstairs to buy some drinks from the vending machines. A cute little boy, who looked about the age of a first-grader, had put his money in the machine, but he hadn't received his juice drink. Tears shone in his eyes, touching Eiko's heart. She immediately offered to help, noticing that the machine showed he still owed a hundred-yen coin. Eiko placed the necessary coin in the slot, and out came the juice box.

The little boy smiled, bowed, and thanked her three times.

Grandmother commented on how polite he was. "He must have good parents," she said with conviction.

The ladies sipped their cold cans of ocha, and soon the guys joined them. They all decided they would pass on the massage chairs in order to go up to their room for dinner. Grandma and Mother immediately lay down on their soft futons, while Eiko touched up her hair.

By the time Eiko finished, her stomach was beginning to growl. At check-in, they had asked for their dinner to be brought to their room. She hoped it would arrive soon.

A knock at the door told her their food had indeed arrived. Eiko quickly opened the door and directed the three women in beautiful kimonos to set everything on the two low tables, set up end-to-end, in the middle of the room. Eiko set out five *zabuton*, or floor cushions, to mark where they would sit.

The women in kimonos had brought the food on trays, which they placed on the tables, making Eiko's mouth water as she took in the beautiful display. Included in the feast was a freshly grilled fish, some tasty mountain vegetables, a large bowl of miso soup, and a bowl of white sticky rice, along with a few Japanese pickles in a tiny square dish.

The two men joined them, and they all sat down around the tables. After saying *itadakimasu* in unison—"we humbly receive this feast"—they began eating their delicious and healthy meal. Soon they were satisfied and began talking about the old days, when they were on trips with Yu's and Eiko's papa.

Yu brought up one such trip years before, when he and Eiko were in elementary school. "Do you guys remember going on a summer vacation to the island of Honshu, in the mountains outside of the Tokyo area? The small Japanese inn came highly recommended. It had been built slightly more than a hundred years before, and had been well cared for by the owners through the generations."

Etsuko picked up his story and continued. "Wasn't that the inn that had a lot of big tarantula-type spiders living in the high wooden beams in the ceiling?"

"Yes, it was," Eiko answered. "They came out at night from their hiding places and walked among us." Eiko's body shivered at that memory.

"I do recall how scared you were, Eiko," Grandma added, "and how you kept on screaming and would not fall asleep."

Yu jumped in to finish the tale. "Father told you a story he made up, about the family of harmless spiders who had lived at the inn for decades. He used different voices for each of the spiders, according to their ages. You fell asleep when he was telling you about their adventures. Ha!"

Everyone chuckled, especially Eiko, as they all agreed that Papa was a fun person to be around. He made life better for others because of his sweet spirit.

"And what about Uncle Yoshi?" Yu asked. "He wanted to be a doctor, right?"

Eiko smiled, as she listened to the comfortable family discussion. Yes, Uncle Yoshi, Papa's older brother, had wanted to be a doctor, but instead had been killed in a car accident right after he graduated from college. Everyone seemed to focus on his kind heart and how he had wished to help people.

After their dinner and several cups of ocha, the men got up and placed the tables closer to the door. They knew the ladies in kimonos would soon return to pick up the trays.

The guys went back to their room to watch a little TV, while the ladies got in under their warm futon covers. Eiko could tell from their deep, even breathing that both her mother and grandmother had fallen asleep quickly. It wasn't long before she joined them. At some point in the night, the trays were retrieved, but Eiko didn't hear a sound.

The next morning, Eiko awoke to find that the trays had been retrieved, though she hadn't heard a sound during the night. She and her mother and grandmother for dressed and went down to the dining area to eat breakfast, which consisted of a buffet with lots of choices that pleased everybody. Uncle Kenta and Yu were already there to greet them.

Grandma smiled as she looked at all the different kinds of fruit. Yuitsu announced how happy he was to discover several types of coffee and teas.

They each filled their plates and sat down at a large table, where they did more talking than eating. Some of them even returned for seconds, but all left happy and full.

Returning to their rooms, they packed their bags and put their futons and covers back in the closet, while they placed their dirtied linens in a pile on the tatami floor. They lounged around in their rooms until the eleven a.m. check-out time.

Just before heading downstairs to pay their bill, Eiko heard a friendly knock. Etsuko, who was closest to the door, slid it open.

"I came to get your bags and take them downstairs," Yu announced.

Mother showed him where they were and thanked him for his thoughtfulness.

Once their bill was paid, the guys made their way outside, while the women waited inside, where it was warm. The men put the luggage in the cars, then let the vehicles idle with the heaters turned on. By the time they climbed in and drove to the front entrance to pick up the ladies, the temperature inside the cars was cozy and comfortable.

When they reached the base of the mountains, they stopped at a roadside tourist restaurant to order soba, a traditional soup enjoyed on New Year's Eve. Eiko thought it was the perfect ending to their fun, family trip. Everyone was in a good mood and had light hearts...but that was to change very quickly.

As soon as they got home, they began to prepare for their New Year's Eve traditions. Uncle Kenta announced that everyone would be going to the temple for the bell ringing, but things didn't go as easily or as well as he seemed to think they would. Grandma said she didn't want to get out so late, for fear she might get chilled. Etsuko said she was still too grief-stricken to go. Yu said he was too tired, and Eiko simply said she didn't want to go.

Uncle Kenta frowned. "Eiko, what is up? I thought for sure I could count on you to go with me. You have always loved going to the temple for the bell ringing. I remember how fascinated you were to hear the bell ring. You remember, do you not? The bell rings 108 times for each known sin, according to Buddhist belief. You used to ask me every year what the bell ringing symbolized, and I told you it helps us by getting rid of our sins before the New Year begins. The bells ring out before midnight, with the final one ringing exactly at one minute past midnight to celebrate New Year's Day. Somehow, even as a young elementary school girl, you could always stay up till midnight for such an event. What has happened that you do not wish to do so this year?"

"I know, Uncle Kenta. I remember. But this year is different." She took a deep breath. "I am a Christian now. My heart beats for Jesus Christ. He has become my Friend, and I have become His. He is my Savior and Lord, and I do not need to get forgiveness from anyone else but Him."

Her uncle's eyes widened, and his mouth fell open. "What? I cannot believe this foolishness is coming from your mouth! Who has brainwashed you and told you Japanese ways are bad? Tell me, and I will have a word with him or her!"

When no one spoke up, Eiko said, "If you only knew Jesus, you would understand."

Uncle Kenta shook his head. "No. I will never understand that thinking. We Japanese worship the sun goddess, who created our people to live on these islands. The Shinto gods have lived among us as emperors for thousands of years." He nodded now. "Yes, yes. We Japanese understand who is for us."

Eiko was determined to press ahead. "Almighty God is for you, Uncle Kenta. He loves all of the world's people. The Bible says in John 3:17, 'God did not send his Son into the world to judge the world guilty, but to save the world through him.' Almighty God's one and only Son, Jesus Christ, who is perfect and holy, laid down His life on the Cross for each of us."

Her uncle's face was red with rage, as he spat out, "That is garbage. You do not know what you are talking about. It is all lies."

Eiko politely excused herself and went up to her room. She lay on her bed next to Kiku, who had run upstairs after her. The tears began to flow, and she didn't even try to stop them. She didn't feel like praying; she was numb. Eiko had never seen her uncle in this kind of rage. Why had he verbally abused her? Was it because she spoke the name of Jesus Christ to him? She listened to Kiku's purring noises, and the slow, steady rhythm helped to quiet her.

If only Yu had stood up for her. She already knew her Mother wouldn't, but why not her grandmother? *Why did*

Grandma not protect me from Uncle Kenta's verbal abuse? He is her son, after all. Eiko felt a wave of self-pity roll over her. What should she do now? *If only Papa was still alive. He would not have let his older brother do that to me. Oh, Papa, I miss you so!*

At that moment, Eiko realized she needed God's help, and so she prayed, aloud but softly. "Lord, I was not prepared for this battle today. I only wanted Uncle Kenta to know You, instead of relying on a religious philosophy or gods made by human hands. Why is he so afraid to talk about You, to hear about You, and to see You alive in me? Please guide my thoughts, and bring me understanding in your perfect timing. Amen."

Eiko's tears soon stopped, as she found herself thinking of the three monkey carvings in the temples. One represented speak no evil, another one, hear no evil, and the last one, see no evil. Was that the enemy's clever warning about staying away from any contact with Christianity? Could that explain Uncle Kenta's severe reaction to hearing, seeing, and speaking about the Good News of Jesus Christ? Was he bound up in total fear?

Wada san, the college minister at her church in Tokyo, had shared his own thoughts about this subject. *He told us that many brave and committed Japanese Christians were martyred for their faith in the 1600's, dying horrible deaths. Sadly, historical events like that have a way of being left out of school textbooks. Not many know how brave the Japanese believers were to honor Almighty God with their deaths.*

Some believers wanted to avoid such torturous deaths, so they denied their faith in public by stomping on an image of Jesus Christ. Other followers of Christ went underground to avoid capture or death. In the years that followed, the underground church became weak, and the truth about God was compromised.

It was almost too painful to think about how the martyrs suffered and died, but it touched Eiko's heart to know what they went through to ensure that, in the future, others would be able to know God and experience His love. As Wada san had explained to the group, Christians need to share the Good News of Jesus without fear, because what happened in the past has no bearing on them today.

Eiko yawned several times. She got up and opened her dresser drawer to get out a pair of pajamas, deciding on her Ling Ling giant panda pajamas, which she had purchased at Ueno Zoo earlier in the year, when Ling Ling had been gifted to Japan by China. With happy thoughts about Ling Ling's cuteness and sweet personality, she turned off the light and got into bed, even though it was close to dinnertime. *I am not hungry. Tomorrow, when I wake up, it will be a New Year—1994. I wonder if it is going to be a year of disappointments and personal problems....*

When morning came, Eiko wanted to stay in bed, so she did. Mother soon came to check on her and to tell her it was time to get up. Eiko told her mother she wasn't feeling well and would come down later. Etsuko let the cat out of Eiko's room and closed the door behind her.

An hour or so later, Yu came knocking. "Eiko, may I come in for a few minutes?"

"I'm not really up to it, Yu," she called out.

"I will not stay long," Yu pleaded.

She sighed. "Okay. Come in."

As Yu stepped into the room, Eiko could see the compassion on his face as he looked at her. She knew her eyes were swollen and her cheeks red from crying so much the night before, so there was no sense pretending all was well.

"I do not know anything about Jesus," he said, "except for what you have told me about Him. But I think that if Uncle Kenta did to Jesus what he did to you, Jesus would be downstairs right now talking to him and showing Him God's love. Is that what you think, too?"

Eiko felt a flush creep up her neck to her face. "Well... that sounds right, I guess," she admitted. "But I am not Jesus. You know that, silly."

Yu flashed her his most irresistible smile. "But you are a Jesus-follower, and you said you are so grateful to Him for saving you. What about it? Will you face Uncle Kenta in order to love him for Jesus' sake and make things right in the family once again?"

Tears threatened to overflow onto her cheeks. "You are right, Yu. But I will need some time to get ready."

"No problem. See you in a little while."

Eiko took a hot shower and got dressed. She picked up her New Testament Bible and chose to read John 3:17, and to think about its meaning. If Jesus wasn't sent to the world to condemn it but to save it, as the verse declared, how could Eiko condemn anyone, especially a family member? She prayed, asking the Lord to forgive her for acting childish when Uncle Kenta questioned her and insulted her faith. She also prayed for more patience and strength to do the right thing. *And, Lord, thank You for sending Yu to comfort me and help me out. I love You, Lord.*

At last she descended the stairs and walked into the kitchen, greeting the family with genuine kindness. She was greatly relieved when they reacted kindly to her, as well.

"Happy New Year! Akemashite omedetou gozaimasu," they all said to each other.

She sat down and had some breakfast, while everyone else waited for her to finish before going into the living room. After that, sitting in front of a roaring fire, they planned their day. Uncle Kenta said he wanted to take Estuko and Grandma to the temple to buy the special good-luck fortune scroll and an arrow to ward off evil in the New Year. He also asked if they knew where last year's arrow was, and Mother said it was put way in the tatami room. It was a custom at the end of each year to take the old arrow back to the temple for it to be burned. Then a new arrow could be purchased for the New Year.

The day before Uncle Kenta and Grandma were to leave was the last official holiday of the New Year. The two of them decided to go out with Etsuko and make a few visits to neighbors and friends, like Fumiko, a sweet lady Eiko's family had known for fifty years, and who now lived in an assisted living facility. Eiko had visited her the morning of Papa's wake.

Since it was Yu's last day off from work, and the local ski resorts were open, with a nice base of snow, Eiko challenged him to go skiing with her, and he agreed. They got their ski equipment out of the storage closet and drove over in about forty minutes. They put on their ski boots before getting out of the car, then carried the skies on one shoulder, as they walked from the car to the ticket shack. After paying for their passes and hooking them on their jacket zippers, they were set to wait in line to ride the ski lift up the mountain. Eiko and Yu decided to do medium-level runs.

Eiko had expected a much longer wait, but there were fewer people than expected, so over the next several hours, they were able to ski down the mountain many times before deciding to head back home.

"It was great fun, Yu. Arigatou! Thank you so much!"

Yu nodded. "Yes, it was, Eiko. I cannot believe you can still keep up with me."

She laughed. "Well, living on my own in Tokyo has made me stronger. Do you think you will ever try living there?"

He shook his head. "No. I feel a responsibility to stay close to Mother. Since her parents died years ago and now Papa is also gone, she has no one close by to watch out for her except me. And besides, I actually love living in Sapporo. If I stayed here my whole life, I would be happy. I know you want to be in Tokyo, and that is fine, as long as you come home to visit us regularly."

"I will, Yu." She nodded emphatically. "I promise. And maybe you can come to Tokyo to visit me. I would love for you to meet my friends, the Sakamotos. Remember I told you about them? They own the fish market in my neighborhood. I also want you to meet Sayuri and Satoh kun. I think you would really like them."

Yu smiled. "Who knows, Eiko? I might actually make it there one day."

She changed the subject then. "Are you going to be okay, Yu?" Eiko was still worried about his excessive alcohol drinking. "I mean, about being stressed out and what you choose to do when you have too much stress in your life."

Eiko could tell her brother was feigning surprise. "Who's stressed out? Me? Do I look stressed out to you?"

She eased up a bit. "No. You look pretty relaxed after a day of skiing. Will you promise to call me when you are overwhelmed at work or at home, trying to help mother with her grief, and it all gets to be too much for you?"

His jaw twitched. "I will, Eiko. *Goshimpai naku.* Do not worry."

When they arrived home, they stood their skis up in the corner of the carport and went inside to find a nice fire in the fireplace. The weather had remained in the teens all day, but the sky was a beautiful *nihonbare*, sunny and clear. "It would have been *taihen*, an awful day, if there had been a blizzard," she observed.

"That is for sure," Yu agreed.

CHAPTER FIVE

Eiko had mixed emotions about having only three days left before returning to Tokyo. She had enjoyed meeting Mari for donuts the day Uncle Kenta and Grandma went home. Now, even though she missed her job and her friends in Tokyo, she wanted to go skiing one more time. She couldn't go with Yu because he was working. She considered calling a friend she hadn't seen in a while, but opted not to, deciding instead to go by herself to the same ski resort where she and Yu had been only a few days before. She rode public transportation, got her ski-lift ticket, and was on the slopes in less than an hour from the time she'd left home.

Eiko had great runs for several hours, until the crowds started to arrive. Several children had shown up by then, many young and all anxious to try out their new ski equipment or ski fashions they had bought with their *otoshidama*, a one-time-a-year special gift of money, given at the beginning of the New Year by adults to the children in their family. The kids could be reckless on the slopes, especially when it was crowded, so Eiko decided to do one more run and then call it a day.

She chose a medium-level course, emptying down into a wide beginner's run that went right down to the lodge. As she skied into the beginners' area, she proceeded with great caution, doing her best to avoid little children who had little or no training. Things went well until, seemingly out of nowhere, a preschool-aged child, moving at a snail's pace, ended up crossing right in front of Eiko. She had to make a snap decision to keep the child safe, so she made a quick turn to her left and missed running into the child, who never noticed anything was wrong. Eiko, on the other hand, twisted her ankle in the process, which caused her to lose her balance and fall, ending up with her left ski in an awkward position. When her momentum stopped, she knew her left leg was broken. The pain was excruciating, causing her to gasp for breath. A kind, older gentleman spotted her and assessed the situation, then skied down to the lodge to alert the ski patrol. Two sympathetic women stayed with Eiko, while she waited for help. The tall one removed her skis and stuck them in the snow, forming an "x" so skiers would go around the hazard. The shorter woman crouched down on her skis to speak encouragingly to Eiko.

"Help is coming," the woman assured her. "It will not be long now."

Eiko moaned. She appreciated the woman's efforts, but they didn't change her situation. "My leg hurts so badly. Please help me...."

"Help is coming," the woman repeated." It won't be long. Try to stay calm."

As Eiko lay on her back, she gazed at the sky. Clouds had come in and hidden the sun. She shivered, remembering the fun she'd had, skiing with her brother just the other day. *If only the little child had not skied right in front of me...* Eiko closed her eyes to rest them a while.

The noise of a snowmobile caught her attention, as it approached from the direction of the lodge. In moments, she spotted two safety ski patrols carrying a stretcher and hurrying in her direction. They stopped, put down the stretcher, and approached the snowmobile driver, who Eiko soon learned was a medic. Kneeling down beside her, the medic carefully strapped an air-filled stabilizer around her left leg. The other men gently picked her up and laid her on the stretcher. Each move, regardless of how careful the men tried to be, sent stabs of pain through Eiko's leg. It was all she could do not to scream.

Once the men had secured Eiko on the stretcher, they skied her down to the lodge area. An ambulance was parked nearby, lights on and waiting, and she was quickly loaded inside to be taken to Sapporo Hospital.

The ambulance attendants asked for information from Eiko, as they tried to make her comfortable. "What is your name? Where do you live? What is your telephone number?"

Eiko was able to give them some basic information, including her mother's home phone number, and that was relayed to the hospital.

Once at the hospital emergency room, Eiko was assigned to the doctor on call. Studying his face, Eiko thought he looked familiar, but she knew her thoughts were muddled by the pain of her injury. Meanwhile, the medical staff assessed her injuries and ordered x-rays.

Eiko asked a nurse to call her mother and was told she had already been contacted.

"*Goshimpai naku,* do not worry," the nurse assured her. "We are taking good care of you. Your mother will be here soon." Eiko was still in the emergency room when her mother arrived and was allowed in to see her.

Etsuko's face was pale and drawn. "Eiko, what happened? You are such an excellent skier."

"I turned too quickly to avoid skiing into a little child, who was floundering in front of me," she explained. "I twisted my ankle and fell down in a precarious position. It was just an unusual accident, Mom. I believe God is a loving God, and He will help me heal. The doctor has not said much. Hopefully, he will let me know something soon. They are looking at my x-ray results now."

"If your God was more loving, maybe you would not have fallen."

Mother's words stung Eiko's heart, but she did not respond, choosing instead to ask about her brother. "Does Yu know what happened?"

Etsuko shook her head. "No. I did not think I should bother him at work. When he gets home, I will tell him."

Eiko winced in pain as she tried to move her injured leg. *Oh, God, please help me endure this pain!* The doctor had explained that he didn't want to give her any pain medication until he knew the extent of the injury. Eiko explained that to her mother, who appeared concerned but didn't say anything more about it.

A nurse came to Eiko then and asked if she had heard a crunch when she fell.

"I do not remember hearing a specific sound," she said. "I just knew it was broken."

"Okay." The nurse nodded. "The doctor will be in soon to talk with you."

In a few minutes, a new doctor walked in and spoke to Eiko and Etsuko. He introduced himself as Dr. Honda, an orthopedic surgeon. "You have fractured your leg above your ankle and torn the ligaments around your ankle when you sprained it. We need to do surgery to repair the fracture and secure the ligaments."

Eiko's heart began to race. "But I do not live in Sapporo. I need to get back to Tokyo and my life there. How long will it take before I am allowed to travel?"

The doctor's facial expression turned more serious. "You will be in hospital for at least five weeks and will need physical therapy at home for another three weeks after that. And, of course, that is if everything goes well. If not, it could be longer."

Eiko felt her eyes tear up. This was almost too much to bear. She was glad she would be able to spend more time with Mother and Yu, but she was also looking forward to returning to her happy and thriving life in Tokyo.

"When will you do the surgery?" Eiko managed to ask.

"I have you scheduled for tomorrow afternoon, about four p.m. You will stay in the ER until then."

Eiko's heart twisted. "Please, I need to make a few calls to Tokyo before my surgery, and I cannot get to one of the public phones in the lobby. Is there some way for me to do that here, in the ER?"

The doctor nodded. "Yes. We can bring in a phone with an outside line. I will tell the nurse that you need one. Also, the ER doctor will check on you tonight and tomorrow before you are transported to the surgery floor. I will see you then."

Mother leaned over Eiko's bed and straightened her blanket. "I am going to go home now and gather some items for you. Is there anything special you need that I might not think of?"

"Yes. I need my Bible. It is on my bed. Would you bring it, please?" Eiko hesitated a minute. There was something else she wanted, but she wasn't sure if now was the time to bring it up. Then again, what better time could there be? "Mother, have you found the package that Uncle Yoshi's best friend left at the house for me when he visited you in December? He said it belonged to Papa."

Etsuko appeared a bit flustered. "I have not found that, not yet. I moved it out of your room because Kiku tore some of the packaging, remember? You know how inquisitive Siamese cats are. I will try to find it soon."

Mother said her goodbyes then, and Eiko closed her eyes to rest. Suddenly the events of the day made her so sleepy, and she dozed in and out for the next couple of hours. She woke up feeling a little hungry and asked the middle-aged nurse if she could have something.

"Since you are having surgery tomorrow, you may have only liquids until midnight. I have some box juices. I will bring you two or three."

"Thank you," Eiko said meekly. "I have never had surgery, so I do not know what to expect."

The nurse chuckled. "After this, you will be a pro."

That chuckle does not sound very encouraging, Eiko thought to herself. *It sounded like she believes it is going to be more difficult than I could ever imagine. Lord, please help me to trust You for all of my needs, physical and emotional. Thank You for walking with me, through good times and bad. Amen.*

In the evening, the ER doctor came to check on Eiko. This time Eiko studied his face and quickly remembered who he was—her papa's doctor. She remembered how young he looked, as he cared for her beloved father. She also recalled her mother, chiding her, when Eiko expressed concern at his youth. Etsuko had told her he was the best in his field. As it turned out, he took care of her papa throughout his illness—from the time he had collapsed at work, through the time he remained in a coma, and right up until his death.

"I am pretty sure we have met," Eiko ventured. "You are Dr. Suzuki, right? You were my papa's doctor right before he passed away."

The pleasant looking gentleman smiled. "Yes, I am Dr. Suzuki. Was your father in a coma? And you live in Tokyo, yes? I remember well."

"Yes, he was, and yes, I do."

The doctor examined Eiko's leg and spoke sympathetically. "*Taihen deshou.* You are probably feeling awful about your circumstances right now."

"Yes. I wish it had not happened, but I am a Christian, and I have God walking with me, both in good times and bad. I know He will help me pull through. I trust Him."

"Have you been a follower of Christ for many years?"

"No. It has only been since my papa's death." She took a deep breath and forged ahead. "How about you? Are you a follower of Christ?"

The kind doctor nodded. "Actually, I am. I was about your age when I trusted in Jesus as my Savior and Lord. Medical school was a challenge that almost got the best of me, but God guided me through successfully. I owe everything to Him."

Eiko was puzzled. "How can you do this job when your patients do not improve, or when some die, like my papa?"

"I do the best I know how and let God take care of the rest," he said thoughtfully. "I do pray for each of my patients while I am treating their illnesses."

Eiko was quiet then, thinking about what the doctor had said. After a brief pause, he asked, "You know your surgery is scheduled tomorrow afternoon with Dr. Honda, right? Do you have any questions or concerns that you want me to answer before that?"

She thought for a moment. "Dr. Honda said I will not be able to return to Tokyo for at least eight weeks. I am disappointed that it takes that long." Eiko blinked back her tears.

"Well, our legs are important," the doctor said with a smile. "The hope and plan is to keep them working well our entire lives. Things happen, and some people do not have the freedom or blessing of having healthy legs. In your case, if the healing is rushed or incomplete, it could become a problem that stays with you a long time. The ligaments are torn around your ankle, and you have a fracture above your ankle. That is a significant injury."

Eiko sighed. "I love to go on hikes and nature walks. I also love to ski. Will I be able to do those things again?"

With raised eyebrows Dr. Suzuki responded, "As I said, it depends on your healing, but you most likely will be able to do those things again, including skiing."

The doctor wrote some notes in Eiko's file, then left to check on the other patients in the emergency room. Eiko felt very blessed to have met another Christian. *I would never have thought Dr. Suzuki was a Christian. When he was treating Papa, he seemed so serious, almost uncaring. God, thank You for surprising me with that God-conversation. I remember the Bible says in John 3:16, "whosoever" believes in Jesus receives His gift of salvation and eternal life—living with Him forever in heaven. Dr. Suzuki is a "whosoever," and I am, too. We are all "whosoevers."*

Eiko fell asleep then, waking up intermittently when the nurses checked her vital signs and looked in on her. The morning dawned, and Eiko was hungry but unable to eat because of her scheduled surgery. She wondered when her mother planned to come to the hospital with her things.

She looked around and listened, realizing the emergency room was still very busy this morning. Eiko could see some of the patients, who had been brought in by ambulances, before they went around the corner and out of her sight. Eiko's thoughts turned to those people and what possible crisis each had experienced. She felt compelled to say a prayer for each of them.

Around nine o'clock in the morning, a middle-aged nurse with a ponytail, whom Eiko had seen the day before, showed up again. As she passed by Eiko's bed and greeted her, Eiko called softly to her, keeping her voice low so as not to disturb the other patients.

"Excuse me, but yesterday I asked about making a few phone calls to Tokyo before my surgery. The doctor said a phone with an outside line could be brought in to me. Please, may I use it now?"

The nurse smiled. "Sure. I can get it for you in just a few minutes."

True to her word, the nurse brought the phone to her almost immediately. Before she could us it, Eiko had to agree to the rules: #1 No loud voices; #2 No more than five minutes per phone call; #3 No more than five calls; #4 A charge of $5 per call would be added to her hospital bill, up to $25 total. Eiko readily signed the agreement and picked up the receiver.

She first called her employer's office, and his assistant answered. Eiko explained that she had injured her leg while skiing and would be having surgery this afternoon to repair it. She mentioned that she still had about three days left of her time off, but was now facing an eight-week recovery in Sapporo before she could return to Tokyo and her job at the company. The assistant said "*Odaiji ni,* please take care. I will inform Mr. Itoh, and we will be in contact with you through your Sapporo contact information."

Next, Eiko called Sayuri's home phone and left a message, since she was at work. Afterward, she called Satoh and did the same thing. She regretted not being able to hear their voices and have a conversation with them, but it would be difficult to say much in the allotted five minutes per call.

The Sakamotos, who owned the local fish market in Eiko's neighborhood and who had become family to her, were her fourth call. Mrs. Sakamoto answered the phone, "Moshi moshi," to which Eiko responded, "Ohayou gozaimasu. Good morning. This is Eiko calling from Sapporo." After informing Mrs. Sakamoto of her latest news, she had a favor to ask.

"I am so happy that I gave you a key to my apartment before I left on vacation. Would you please check my mailbox weekly and put it all in my *genkan,* the entryway? And arigatou, thank you, for watering my two plants during the New Year holidays. Would you please keep watering them until I return home?"

Mrs. Sakamoto told her several times not to worry and how they would anxiously await her return, putting many of Eiko's concerns at rest.

The final call Eiko decided to make was to her mother. The phone rang several times before Etsuko picked up. "Mom, it is me. How are things going? When are you planning on coming to the hospital?"

"I almost have everything ready. I am planning to leave in about forty-five minutes. I talked to your brother after he got home from work last night. He said he would get permission to leave work early today, perhaps even getting to the hospital before your surgery. If not, Eiko, he will certainly be there when you wake up afterward."

Eiko smiled. "Oh, that is nice of Yu." *That makes me so happy. Yu is once again acting like he enjoys being my big brother, like he used to when we were growing up.*

"I know your phone time is limited," Etsuko said, "so I will say goodbye now. Oh, one more thing. I have your Bible packed with your things, so I will bring it when I come."

Eiko couldn't help but smile. She was already feeling a bit more hopeful.

Chapter Six

Mother arrived at the hospital just in time to see her daughter moved from the ER to the surgical wing. The nurse told Eiko's mother that she needed to borrow Eiko for a while, so she could get examined and prepped for surgery, even though it was still three hours away. The nurse suggested Etsuko wait in the large family waiting room, with the promise that she would be invited back behind closed doors to sit with Eiko one hour before her surgery.

Just as she'd promised, around 3 p.m., the nurse came out to the family waiting room to invite Etsuko to follow her to Eiko's pre-surgery room. When she arrived, Eiko looked pleased to see her.

Etsuko went straight to her daughter's bedside. "Hello, dear. How are you doing?"

"I am so tired and very hungry," she said, "but I am ready to get this behind me. I am glad there is only one hour left. The surgeon told me it might take as long as three hours to do the surgery. After I get out of the recovery area, I will be getting a private room for a short time. Then I will be moved into a room with three other patients, who have all had orthopedic surgery or concerns."

Etsuko nodded. "Well, I have your small bag with me right now. I will bring it to you when you get to your private room after recovery."

"Can you get out my Bible now, Mom? And hand it to me, please."

Mother reached into the small pink duffle bag and brought it out.

Eiko smiled as she took it in her hands. "Thank you. I want to read it for a few minutes. Do you mind? Would you like for me to read it out loud so you can hear it, too?"

Etsuko felt she had no choice, so she mumbled a resigned "yes."

Eiko turned to Matthew 4 and began reading at verse 23. "Jesus went everywhere in Galilee, teaching in the synagogues, preaching the Good News about the kingdom of heaven, and healing all the people's diseases and sicknesses. The news about Jesus spread all over Syria, and people brought all the sick to him. They were suffering from different kinds of diseases. Some were in great pain, some had demons, some were epileptics and some were paralyzed. Jesus healed all of them. Many people from Galilee, the Ten Towns, Jerusalem, Judea, and the land across the Jordan River followed him."

Eiko closed her New Testament Bible and smiled at her mother. "I am encouraged to read God's truth that Jesus is our Healer. He had the power over every disease and sickness then, and He still has that power. He heals because of His compassionate heart for each of us. He loves us and wants us to experience His love in powerful ways."

Etsuko felt confused at what she'd heard, but she was curious too. "How did you know where to find that particular scripture?"

"I have read the entire book of Matthew," Eiko answered. "More than once, actually. That is how I remembered where it was." She handed the Bible back to her mother, who tucked it away in Eiko's bag at her feet.

Etsuko waited for several minutes before she changed the subject. "By the way, Kiku is lonely for you. When she saw me packing a few of your clothes, I think she tried to hide in the bag to come see you. She is so smart."

"Why do you not let her sleep in your bed with you while I am in the hospital? She has been sleeping in your bed since I moved to Tokyo, right?"

Etsuko sighed. "I suppose so. But when you are home, she forgets about me."

Eiko patted her mother's hand. "Well, now you will get her company for five weeks."

A nurse entered the room to inform them that it was almost time for Eiko to receive her anesthesia. This time it was Etsuko's turn to touch Eiko's hand. "See you when it is over." Then the nurse politely led Etsuko back out to the family waiting room.

Etsuko had been sitting and waiting for Yu for nearly an hour. When she looked up and saw that he had arrived, she watched, as he looked for a seat, but there were too many family members waiting for their loved ones in surgery. After a moment of scanning the room, he went and stood by his mother and leaned down to ask about Eiko.

"It is nice to see you," Etsuko said, in answer to his question. "Arigatou for coming. Eiko's surgery is just starting. She will probably be a few hours yet. Shall we go down to the dining room to get some dinner?"

Yu shrugged. "I guess so, if that is what you want to do."

After letting the nurse at the desk know where they were going, they found the elevator and went down to the basement floor to get to the cafeteria. It was not that crowded, so they walked right in, found something they wanted, and paid for it at the cashier's booth. They found a table for two and sat down. Though Etsuko's heart longed to discuss the situation with Yu, she thought it better to let him eat in silence. They could talk about Eiko afterward.

When they finished eating, Yu asked Mother to fill him in. Mother told him about the examination and preparation Eiko had to do beforehand, adding that Eiko definitely felt tired and very hungry. "Her special request of me was to bring her Bible to the hospital, which seemed to bring her some peace. The section she read out loud was all about Jesus being our Healer."

When Yu nodded but didn't speak, Etsuko changed the subject. "I thought Eiko was an excellent skier, Yu. Why did this happen?"

"From the information I have gathered, it was just a freak accident," he explained. "A little child, oblivious of the danger, got in her way. Eiko made a quick decision to turn sharply, and it sprained her ankle, which kept her from recovering her balance. Her left ski was not in a good position to land at that angle. I personally think of her as a hero for not running into the child."

Etsuko smiled and nodded. "If you say so, dear." She glanced at the large clock on the wall. "Let us get back to the family waiting room and check at the information desk to see if there is any news—though I doubt there will be yet."

When they arrived at the waiting room, there were fewer people than before, so they would have plenty of seats to choose from. Before they sat down, Yu and his mother went up to the desk and asked for information about Eiko. The nurse standing nearby said she would go back and see if she could obtain any information for them. They waited until she returned, and then they stepped closer to the counter to hear what she had to say.

"The doctor will be out in about twenty minutes to discuss it with you," she explained, without giving them any real information

Etsuko and Yu sat down and waited. Not quite half an hour later, they both stood up when they saw the doctor enter the room.

Dr. Honda nodded when he saw them. "Eiko's injury was more complex than the x-rays showed. In addition to the main fracture, there was another hairline fracture, hidden behind one of her torn ligaments. She has many stitches on the inside, as well as on the outside. It will be slow going to regain the use of her leg, but if she works hard during her hours of physical therapy, she has a very good chance at a full recovery."

Etsuko thanked him for doing the surgery. He told them it would take about thirty more minutes before Eiko would be taken to her own room, and then he left. About a half-hour later, the lady at the desk called them over. "Eiko is in room #307. As you leave the waiting area, turn right and then make the first left. Down the long hallway there will be directions to her wing. Follow the signs from there."

"Thank you," Etsuko said gratefully, turning to smile at Yu. He too appeared relieved.

They followed the woman's directions and soon walked into the private room, where a nurse tried to help Eiko find a comfortable position for her left leg. Etsuko noticed it was wrapped in an air-filled stabilizer, no doubt to protect it from being bumped and to provide support. It could be taken off simply by pulling the Velcro straps free.

Etsuko and Yu waited patiently, until the nurse stepped back and Eiko was able to see them. "What perfect timing," she said, her voice weak but encouraging.

Eiko glanced at them and did her best to offer a smile. "Hi," she murmured. "I guess it is over."

Mother and Yu stepped closer to her bed, as the nurse excused herself and left.

Mother touched Eiko's hand. "Eiko, how are you feeling? Do you remember any of it?"

Eiko thought back, but realized she remembered almost nothing. "All I remember is being so cold. How long did it take?"

"About three hours," Etsuko answered. "They said you have lots of stitches on the inside and outside."

That is why it hurts so badly. Eiko teared up as she thought about it.

"It is over now, Eiko," Yu said. "The worst is over, and now you can start healing. *Goshimpai naku.* Mother and I are here to help you."

Etsuko unpacked her daughter's personal items and placed them in the two drawers provided. Yu left the room on an errand and said he would only be gone a few minutes. When he returned, he had a small, silk floral arrangement in his hands, looking very much like it had just been purchased at the lobby gift shop.

"Arigatou, Yu." Eiko smiled, in spite of the pain. "The silk bouquet of white lilies and greenery is very pretty."

"Yes," Mother agreed. "They are nice."

Eiko dozed in and out, having taken her pain medication when the nurse was with her. The nurse told her she would be in to check on her every two hours. Eiko had also been instructed to push her call button anytime she needed something.

In exactly two hours, the nurse returned and checked Eiko's vital signs. Eiko asked her if she could have something to eat and drink.

"You can have a juice drink and some rice cereal. Would you like that?"

"May I have ocha, please? And some toast?" Eiko's hunger and thirst was growing, and it kept her from sleeping deeply.

"Ocha has too much caffeine," the nurse explained, "and toast will be too heavy on your stomach. Would you like some juice and some warm rice cereal? That is about the best I can offer right now."

Eiko agreed that if she couldn't have the ocha and toast, juice and rice cereal would be fine.

After the nurse left to get those items, Yu and Mother reminded Eiko that it wouldn't be too long before she could eat whatever she wanted. But now her body, especially her stomach, needed to work properly in order for her leg to start healing.

"That is why they want to be careful, Eiko." Yu spoke in a soft, low voice. "The trauma you experienced was intense and invasive."

The two of them stayed with Eiko until she had eaten most of her rice cereal and finished two juice boxes. Then they said goodnight and told her they would see her the next day. She nodded to them as they left, then closed her eyes and quickly fell into a deep sleep.

The first week after the accident was a blur in Eiko's memory. After seventy-two hours, she was moved into a room with four beds. Two were empty, so it was just Eiko and an older lady, who was recovering from knee surgery, in the room together. Before leaving the private room, Eiko learned to get around on crutches so she could take care of her personal needs. She still felt a little wobbly on them, but she was happy to be somewhat independent again. Her meals had progressed to vegetables and a small amount of protein. She also was allowed one cup of coffee or ocha a day, which was a special treat.

Each day her schedule was the same. It included a time where she walked on her crutches and a nurse checked her surgical scar and nearby area for any signs of infection. Each day a new bandage was applied, and also the same protective air-filled stabilizer. In two more weeks, she would no longer need the stabilizer. She then could rely on her own skills to keep her injured area safe from getting bruised as she moved around.

Her roommate, Mrs. Iwamoto, was friendly because they shared a common concern about healing taking place in their legs. The two women tried to encourage one another in their struggles. They each went to physical therapy five times a week and came back exhausted from the workouts. Her roommate's knee injury had been quite extensive, as had Eiko's ankle injury.

Mother continued to come and visit Eiko during the weekdays, and Yu came Saturday and Sunday each week. Both commented to Eiko on how well she seemed to be managing her situation. There had been a few visitors, who heard about her accident and came by to see her. Even Dr. Suzuki stopped in to check on her. But mostly, Eiko missed her friends and church family in Tokyo.

"Eiko san, you look a little down today. Are you in pain?" her roommate asked.

"I am always in pain," she admitted, "so it is not that. I guess I feel blue about not being able to see my friends in Tokyo. I really care for them deeply."

Mrs. Iwamoto smiled. "I have some stationery you can use to write them a letter."

Eiko nodded. "Yes. I think that would help me. Thank you for your kindness." She selected a few sheets and decided to write to Satoh first.

Dear Satoh kun: I miss eating ramen with you at our favorite ramen place by work. But I want you to know that I am enjoying the terrific flavor of my favorite ramen in Sapporo. Wish you could taste it. I know you would agree about how wonderful it is. You might even become a fan.

As I am sure you know, I did not expect to break my leg while I was on vacation. My brother and I had already skied together at this place and had a great time. It was a strange accident, which seemed to have taken place in slow motion and involved a small child. Thank goodness she is all right!

The surgery took about three hours because of the extensive repairs that needed to be done. The doctor said I will continue to have pain as I progress in my physical therapy, until my bone and ligaments are totally healed. Then I will benefit from all of my hard work in therapy, if I do not give up.

How are things with you? Is work going well? How are your cousin Aki and his wife, Yoko? I think about you all and pray for you regularly.

By the way, the first Sunday I was in Sapporo, I went by myself to a church that has lots of young people our age attending. The music is contemporary and is led by a praise band, which includes an electric bass player and a drummer. I really liked it a lot and wished you could have experienced it with me. Maybe someday ... Eiko.

Eiko decided to write Sayuri next.

Dear Sayuri: I miss you, my friend. I know that God is a God of mercy because I have experienced His mercy in the weeks I have been in Sapporo. I really wanted to return to Tokyo to be with everyone at work and church, but God had other things in mind. After a lot of thinking about everything and having conversations with God through prayer, I believe He has extended my time in Sapporo for His purposes. I am reconnecting with my mother and brother. I have made some new friends and have seen God at work in my life and in the lives of others around me.

God blessed me with an encouraging roommate, an older lady who is healing from knee surgery. Please have the church pray for Mrs. Iwamoto's healing. There are four beds in our room, and I wonder if there will be two more ladies joining us soon. This letter is being written on Iwamoto san's stationery, which she generously offered to me.

How was your time in your hometown with your family, whom you have not seen in three years? I prayed that God would protect your heart from any hurt or sadness. I look forward to hearing what took place, if it is something you want to share with me. I also have something I need to share with you about my family time, and also about a church I went to the first Sunday I was here.

Did you watch TV during the New Year holidays, specifically on January 2nd? I watched newlyweds Crown Prince Naruhito and Crown Princess Masako take their places among the Emperor's family to give the general public a traditional New Year's greeting from the Imperial Palace. They looked so happy.

Well, since I am not a princess, I need to put my own things away before lunch arrives. I do get tired of eating in my hospital room. I long to eat out in the park near our workplace. Still over a month left before I get back.

Take care. Your friend ... Eiko.

Eiko folded the two letters and placed them in the envelopes. She quickly wrote the addresses on them and set them aside to give to her mom when she came the next day. Her mood had brightened by remembering her good friends in Tokyo. She handed her roommate the stationery she didn't use, but Iwamoto san insisted she keep it for the next time she engaged in letter-writing. Eiko politely accepted it and said, "Arigatou."

After lunch, Eiko looked forward to her mother's visit. She thought Mother was doing better these days, as her depression seemed to be lifting a little. *Perhaps Mother is feeling that she has found a new purpose for living since Papa's passing. She has put a lot of energy into caring for me, and yet she does not seem weak. Rather, she seems strong and ready for any task.*

Etsuko showed up at 1:30 p.m. and greeted Iwamoto san as she came in and walked over to the chair by Eiko's bed. "Hello, Eiko. You look nice in your long robe. Is it comfortable?"

Eiko smiled. "Thanks, Mom. It is very comfortable, since I cannot have anything tight on my leg yet. In another week, I can wear regular pajamas because my protective stabilizer will no longer be needed. That will be a happy day."

Etsuko nodded. "Yes, I am sure that it will. How was your therapy this morning? Any progress?"

"My physical therapist, Tanaka san, says I am doing okay. I still cannot put any weight on that leg. It is just not ready for that. I practice flexing it and lifting it, from a sitting position. That is supposed to happen before I can finish my recovery at home."

She paused, as her thoughts took a change of direction. "Speaking of home, does Kiku still show signs of missing me? She probably thinks I am already back in Tokyo and forgot to say goodbye."

Etsuko smiled at her daughter's good-natured teasing. "She misses you terribly," she admitted. "She can smell your clothes in your room. She goes in there every day to take a morning nap. She makes some noise that sounds pitiful and then falls asleep on your bed. When she is done, she comes out and joins the family."

Eiko asked her mother to hide a treat under the pillow for Kiku to find each morning. "That will keep her playful and happy," she explained.

Etsuko agreed, then reached down into her purse and brought out two envelopes and a small box of chocolate-covered almonds.

Eiko felt her eyes widen with delight. "Oh, thank you, Mom, for the candy! You know it is my favorite sweet snack." She immediately opened the box and asked her mother if she would like to have one.

"No, dear. They are all yours. Enjoy."

Eiko ate several before realizing she hadn't asked about the envelopes. When she did, her mother handed them to her.

"It is mail that came to the house for you," she explained.

Eiko saw that one envelope was from Mr. Itoh, her boss, and the other was from the Sakamoto family. Eiko opened the letter from Mr. Itoh first and read it out loud.

Dear Eiko san: Please know that we at the company are concerned about your health. We are praying for your recovery. When you are able to return to Tokyo, your job will be waiting for you. You are important to our team. Please let us know of your progress. Sincerely, Mr. Itoh.

"That's very respectable of him," Etsuko observed. "Some bosses do not save jobs when people have to be away for an extended time. You are very fortunate, Eiko. It has proved to be an excellent workplace for your first employment. It is nice that your uncle's best friend's relative, Mr. Itoh, offered you a job."

Eiko nodded. "Yes. It is a miracle, I do believe."

She opened the second letter and read it aloud as well.

Dear Eiko chan: Thank you for calling us the day of your surgery to let us know what happened in your skiing accident. We know you are working hard on your physical therapy in the hospital. We are confident that you will succeed and your leg (and ankle) will be stronger than ever. Enclosed is a pre-paid public telephone card, with a photo of the Tokyo Tower on it. Please use it to call anyone you like. Missing you ... the Sakamoto family.

"How thoughtful they are!" Etsuko exclaimed. "They sound like a sweet family."

"They are," Eiko agreed. "I miss stopping by to see them on my way home from work. I also miss eating dinner with them once a week. God has blessed me with kind friends." She paused a moment and sent up a silent prayer of thanks. *Arigatou, Jesus, for all of the good things You have done for me. I love You.*

CHAPTER SEVEN

Eiko was sad to see Mrs. Iwamoto leave the hospital, but she was also happy that her roommate's knee was healing well enough to go home. She was a kind woman, and Eiko would miss her. Now, with three empty beds in the room, Eiko imagined someone new—or several new people—might be assigned to room #307. She hoped that would happen soon, as she looked forward to having some company.

Eiko was happy that three of the five weeks of her hospitalization were already over. Her ankle and leg were beginning to feel more normal. She was now able to get around on her crutches with skill. The swelling was way down, and her stitches seemed to be fine. And since the air-filled stabilizer around her calf was no longer needed to protect the injury site, Eiko was able to wear her own pajamas from home, rather than the hospital gowns.

With all the snow that had fallen during the last three weeks of January, Eiko would have found it nearly impossible to be out and about on crutches. She understood that, but she was having difficulty accepting it. She loved to be outdoors in the fresh air. She was willing to admit she even missed shoveling snow. She also knew that her family could really have used her help this month. They did have Hiroshi, the high-school aged boy from the neighborhood, shoveling snow for them to earn money for a school trip. Yu and Mother also pitched in when they could. But Eiko wished she too could have helped.

Dismissing that thought, Eiko looked out her hospital window next to her bed, as she did so many times throughout the day. She also gazed out at the winter wonderland from the windows she found along her walks in the hallways. The scenes were so picturesque, almost like postcards.

Eiko was looking forward to today because Yu was coming to visit this afternoon. She appreciated him coming on Saturdays and Sundays, which gave their mother a chance to have two days of rest at home. Yu would usually talk about work or his hobbies. Today he showed up with a medium-sized envelope and a package that had some of the paper torn off. He grinned as she reached for them.

"Are those for me?" Eiko asked, her excitement evident in her tone. "What did you bring me?"

"Actually, is was Mom that asked me to bring them to you. Honestly, I am not sure what they are. Why don't you go ahead and open them? Start with the envelope, okay? That looks interesting. It is postmarked Tokyo."

Eiko opened the envelope after checking the return address. "It is from my co-worker and church friend, Sayuri." She wanted Yu to know who had sent it, even as she dumped the contents out on her bed. She was delighted to find about twenty different greeting cards in envelopes, all from her church family. As she read them, she passed them to Yu to read. Several were funny—most likely to keep her spirits up—and several were sympathetic about the pain she was going through. Each person or family reminded Eiko that they were praying for her and waiting for the day she would be well enough to return to Tokyo. Eiko was pleased to see that Yu seemed impressed that his sister had so many close friends. The cards would not all fit on her bed stand, so she arranged them along the windowsill. She then turned her attention to the somewhat damaged package. It had not come in the mail, so how had it arrived?

Eiko felt her excitement building, as she realized this could be the package her uncle's best friend left for her on a recent trip to Sapporo. It was Papa's, according to what he had told her mother, and he wanted Eiko to have it. It looked about the size of a book, but she wasn't sure. She opened an envelope taped to the top and read it aloud.

Dear Eiko: Your Uncle Yoshi was my best friend in college. I was very sad when he died in an automobile accident after our college graduation. He was a good guy. He had a tender heart toward people. That is why he had a dream of becoming a doctor, but as you know, his life was over before he could pursue that dream. I still think of Yoshi and your family after all these years. I was also your father's friend during my senior year in college, when he was a freshman on our campus.

One thing we three did that year was go to church together. There was a Christian group that met on campus each Sunday. They had guitars and sang melodic songs about Jesus and His love. There were messages from the Bible and lots of fellowship times. During that year, your father, your uncle, and I became followers of Jesus and were baptized. We each received a new Bible and were challenged to read it from cover to cover.

Eiko paused and looked at Yu, to see if he was taking all this in. He appeared perplexed, as if wondering what would come next. Eiko continued reading from where she left off.

I have Yoshi's Bible at my home. He was planning to tell your grandparents about his decision to follow Christ, when he returned to Sapporo after graduation, but sadly, he never made it.

I still have an active faith in Jesus and share God's love on college campuses in my hometown area. I have continued to pray for your family since Yoshi died. I have asked the Lord to open your hearts to the Good News of Jesus Christ. The Lord is the One who gave me the idea of giving you, Eiko, your papa's Bible. I do not know if you are a Christian, but I do know that God planned for you to have it one day. After Yoshi died, your father asked me to hold on to it. He did not know how to deal with the question, "If God is so loving, how could He let a nice young man, like my older brother, die with such a bright future?"

Eiko could not control her emotions. Tears slipped down her cheeks like a swift river in a storm. "Who knew Uncle Yoshi and Papa were Christians? Papa never said anything to us. Why? Why would he not tell us? I do not understand. I *cannot* understand." She looked up at Yu for an explanation, but his head was bent down, as he stared at the floor.

After a moment, Yu looked up, his expression one of disbelief. "Keep on reading the letter, please. Maybe there are some answers written there."

Without further hesitation, she continued. *Please do not be angry with your father or ashamed of him. God loved him so very much. I kept in touch with your father through the years. He made his peace with God about your Uncle Yoshi's sudden death, as he found God's kindness in his grief. Your father told me he hoped to get married one day and have his wife and children go to church every Sunday. That might not have happened, but it was his dream. If anyone in your family becomes a Christian, you will be seeing a loving God answering your father's prayers for his family.*

Eiko continued to weep. Her sweet, devoted papa would be so happy to know she had invited Christ into her heart to be her Savior and Lord. Then God caused her to remember the day when her papa's eyes opened while he was in a coma. She was sitting by his hospital bed, talking about her questions and feelings about Creator God. Could it be that Papa had heard her voice and wanted to encourage her to believe in Almighty God? He had been unable to speak, but their eyes had met briefly.

Eiko squeezed her eyes shut and got lost in her thoughts for a few moments. *God, You are so very kind to have allowed my papa to hear my words and to have allowed me to see my papa's reaction. Oh, the sweet, sweet love of the Lord! How can people turn away from You and not accept the deep love You want to show them?*

Yu interrupted her thoughts. "Are you finished reading the letter?"

Eiko opened her eyes and turned her focus back to the letter. "There is a little more to read. His last paragraph says:

'I want to encourage you, Eiko, that when troubles and trials come into your life, like clouds of gray huddled before a storm, remember to pour out your heart to God in prayer for His help. He will never "leave you or forsake you," as it says in the Bible. You can always count on Him. I am praying for your family. If I can do anything for you, please let me know. My contact information is included below. In Christ's matchless name, Mr. Watanabe.'"

Eiko handed the letter to Yu. He briefly glanced at it, then wordlessly laid it down on her bed.

"What are you thinking, Yu?" she asked, her voice soft. "Did the news Watanabe san shared make God more real to you? Do you want to have faith like our papa?"

Yu hesitated before answering. "Eiko, I am going to have to think some more about what happened this afternoon as you opened Watanabe's letter and began reading. Truthfully, I do not think our family will ever be the same again. This is so much to take in all at once. I will want to talk with Mother about it, too. Would you give me permission to take the letter home and let her read it?"

Eiko nodded. "Of course. Just do not let it get thrown away, okay? I want to treasure it always."

A flicker of a smile crossed Yu's lips. "Thank you, Eiko. I might even call Mr. Watanabe one day and have a talk with him. That was so kind of him to pray for our family all these years."

"I agree. And to think he is the one who recommended me for my job! My boss is related to him. I think Watanabe san was still in contact with Papa last year when I wanted to move to Tokyo and get a job. I bet he helped Papa find a solution to the problem by suggesting his relative's company. It was a prayerful choice because Mrs. Itoh was a believer, and she led Sayuri to Christ before she became my best friend when I went to work there. God is so amazing! It is obvious that His good plan for me and our family started many years ago."

Yu ran his hand through his hair. "He sure loved Uncle Yoshi and our father. I wonder if he ever met Uncle Kenta? Probably not, since Uncle Kenta would have been out of college for several years by then." He paused, then changed the subject. "Eiko, I need something to drink. I am going down to the basement cafeteria and see if I can find something. What should I bring you? What would you like?"

Eiko smiled. "I would like a Fanta orange drink from the soda fountain, please."

"Okay. I will go and be right back," Yu promised as he went out the door.

Eiko got her crutches and walked to the ladies' bathroom down the hallway, wanting to wash the tears from her face. When she returned to her room, she threw the packaging away and picked up her papa's Bible. She saw his name printed on the first page. As she leafed through the already beloved book, she found a bookmark someone had given him on his baptism day, the same day he was presented the Bible. She also found his certificate of baptism. As she flipped through the pages from Genesis to Revelation, she noticed a few scriptures were underlined. *Maybe he, too, like Mr. Watanabe, took on the challenge to read the Bible through from cover to cover.*

Yu walked in then, with the Fanta for Eiko and a cup of coffee for himself. He sat down in the chair by his sister's bed.

Once he was settled, Eiko handed him the Bible. Yu gave it a quick once-over. "Look at some of Father's hand-writing on the inside back cover," he said, holding it out to her so she could see it from her position on the bed. Before she could respond, Yu spoke again, and Eiko recognized the emotion in his voice, though he was obviously doing his best to conceal it. "It is comforting to see Father's Japanese characters written in the traditional calligraphy style. I am impressed with Father's writing skills, as well as his love of learning."

Eiko smiled. "You are so much like our beloved papa. You, too, enjoy studying. Does it make you want to study the Bible as he did?" When Yu didn't answer, Eiko decided to drop the subject.

Eiko was so delighted to have Papa's Bible that she decided to commit to reading the entire thing, no matter how long it took. She slipped it into the top drawer of the bed stand and began drinking her soda.

"Would you like to watch a TV program, Yu?" she asked. "It is Saturday, after all. There are lots of sports shows on."

"Sure," he said, as he used the remote control to search for a program they might enjoy.

Voices interrupted their pursuit of a TV program, and soon several people walked into the room. Two nurses accompanied a teenage patient in a wheelchair, with a female family member by her side. The patient was put in the first bed by the door on Eiko's side. It looked like her arm was bandaged and put in a sling. After the new patient was comfortably situated, the nurses left, but the family member stayed.

Yu's and Eiko's eyes met with a knowing look. "Maybe we should watch a TV program some other time," her brother suggested, setting down the remote. He touched Eiko's arm and told her to rest. "I am going to go home now, Eiko. Would you miss me too much if I did not come for a visit tomorrow? I want to have a talk with Mother during the time I would be here with you. So maybe you can enjoy your day tomorrow reading Papa's Bible. Please pray that Mother will be up to sharing what she knows about Father's faith."

"I will be praying for you and Mother," Eiko assured him, pleased that he had requested prayer. "I will be fine tomorrow. I have a new roommate to get to know. And, of course, getting some information from Mother is something to look forward to." Eiko handed Yu the letter, then stood up and grabbed her crutches. They walked to the door together, and she gave him a brief hug as he waved goodbye and left.

As Eiko turned around to go back to her bed, she noticed the family member was opening the privacy curtain. Eiko decided it was an opportunity to say "hello" to them and introduce herself.

The teenaged patient seemed receptive, and she told Eiko her name was Hana, while the woman identified herself as Hana's mother. After a brief exchange of greetings, Eiko excused herself and got back in bed, with her privacy curtain closed.

Eiko was tired from all the excitement and emotions she had experienced earlier. Now that her leg was doing better, it was easier for her to find a comfortable position in bed.

It also felt so good to be in her own polka-dot pajamas that she quickly fell asleep.

When she awoke, she noticed it was close to dinner-time. About forty minutes later, their meal trays were brought in. Tonight's dinner was fish and fresh vegetables. For dessert there was a *mikan,* a Japanese-style tangerine. Eiko ate most of her dinner and then set it aside. Perhaps her Fanta drink had spoiled her appetite just a bit. Eiko watched TV for an hour, then turned it off and promptly fell back to sleep.

Sometime during the night, before the sun had risen, Eiko woke up to the sound of soft crying. She immediately knew it was coming from her new roommate. Eiko was not sure if Hana's mother was there or if Hana was alone, since the curtain was pulled. But she heard no voices, so after a moment, Eiko asked, "Are you okay? Do you need something? Maybe I can help."

"I am okay," the soft voice responded. "I am just lonely. Can you ... talk to me, Eiko?"

Eiko smiled. "Sure," she said, as she got her crutches and walked around the curtain. The patient's eyes glistened with tears.

"Are you in pain, Hana?" Eiko asked softly.

"No, not really. Just lonely. I do not like hospitals. There are too many rules—like a family member cannot stay in the room at night."

"Oh, I see. Well, I am here, Hana, so you are not alone. I am not a family member, but I can be your friend." She paused to utter a silent prayer and then continued. "You have another Friend named Jesus, who will always be with you and never leave you. He loves everyone in the world. He is Almighty God's one and only Son. He came to earth to show us how much God loves us."

Hana brushed her tears away. "I have never heard about Jesus. He sounds kind."

Eiko nodded. "Yes. He is very kind. May I say a prayer for you? It might help you go back to sleep."

"Okay. You can."

Eiko closed her eyes and bowed her head. "Almighty God, thank You for sending Your one and only Son, Jesus, from heaven to earth to show us how much You love us. I ask You to comfort Hana, that she might feel Your kind love. Please help her get some more sleep so she can get well soon. Amen."

"Arigatou."

"You are very welcome, Hana. Now remember, I am here. And Jesus is here, too, even though we cannot see Him. Goshimpai naku. See you in the morning. Goodnight."

Eiko returned to her bed, and things got quiet in the room once again. The next thing Eiko knew was that the nurses had come in to the start the day. Eiko was pleased to hear the nurse ask Hana if she'd slept well, and the girl replied that she had, thanks to her roommate's prayer.

After breakfast, Eiko began her physical training. Her middle-aged trainer, a man named Tanaka, who had the muscles of an athlete, greeted her and let her know that today's task was for her to take steps, putting weight on her left leg without using crutches.

"We have been practicing with you putting some weight on your left ankle and leg, and you have done well," the trainer said. "But for you to leave the hospital in two more weeks, you have to be able to walk without any crutches. So today is the day your leg will be tested more than it ever has. Come over here to this walkway with guardrails, and let us get started." He held out his hand. "Here, give me your crutches. Begin by putting your hands on the two parallel guardrails. Step first on your right foot, and then try to continue stepping with your left foot."

Eiko put her left foot down gingerly. It did not feel weak, but it did not feel strong either. She made the step with some apprehension, but at least it was a complete step.

"Good," the therapist said, as he then asked Eiko to release her hands from the guardrails so she would be totally standing on her own. Eiko felt a little wobbly after removing her hands, but she was determined to do as the therapist instructed.

"Keep going, and see how far you get," the therapist said. "Only put your hands back on the guardrails if you feel you are going to fall."

With short, sit-down breaks in between, she completed the required forty-five minutes. Eiko could feel herself getting tired. Her last few steps were not as sure or strong as some earlier ones. She realized she must work hard the next two weeks to be able to return home.

Eiko got back to her room in a wheelchair. She was allowed to continue using her crutches, but she was also encouraged to put all her weight down on her left foot as often as possible.

Hana was not in the room when Eiko left for therapy, nor was she there when she returned. *She is probably meeting with her doctor this morning.*

Eiko settled in bed and opened her father's Bible to the book of Psalms, the book in the middle of the Bible. She started with Psalm 1:1, and soon learned that people who love God's Word and who meditate on it day and night are like trees that have a plentiful supply of water, enabling them to bear fruit. She read several of the first psalms and then skipped ahead to Psalm 28:7, reading, "The Lord is my strength and shield. I trust him, and he helps me. I am very happy, and I praise him with my song." In Psalm 29:11, she read, "The Lord gives strength to his people; the Lord blesses his people with peace."

She smiled, closed Papa's Bible, and put it back in the drawer of her night stand. She then gathered the greeting cards from the windowsill. A soft, warm glow filled her heart as she reread them, thinking of all she wanted to say to her friends and church family when she got back to Tokyo. *All I need to do is to walk normally now, without favoring my hurt leg. It is still painful, but in two more weeks, they say the pain will be gone.*

CHAPTER EIGHT

No visitors were allowed in their hospital rooms this early in the day, and the nurses had just left after a routine check-in with the patients, so Eiko and Hana pulled their privacy curtains open and sat on their beds, chatting with one another. Hana seemed to have lots of questions.

"Eiko, how long have you been in hospital?"

"It has been three and a-half weeks now. I have ten days left before I am ready to go home."

The girl's dark eyes widened. "That sounds like a long time. I only have to stay about two weeks, until my shoulder feels better. I hurt it playing basketball at school. They say nothing is broken, but it would be better to recover in hospital rather than go to school every day and take the chance of hurting it more."

Eiko remembered thinking Hana had broken her arm when she first saw her. "So the sling helps with the discomfort?"

Hana nodded. "Yes. The sling helps. I will have physical therapy, too, in order to help regain movement. I hope I do not have to tell my college girls' basketball coach that I will not be able to play the rest of the year."

Hana paused to use her good arm to sweep her long black hair to one side. "Did you go to college, Eiko?"

"Yes. I did. I graduated from university here in Sapporo, but I now live in Tokyo." Eiko thought about how happy she was when her parents made their decision, which allowed her to live on her own in that thriving metropolis.

"I know my parents would never let me do that," Hana stated matter-of-factly.

"Well, my papa wanted it for me more than my mother. But he finally won her over." Eiko thought a moment about her sweet papa. The fact that he was no longer in her life caused her heart to ache. *I miss him so much.*

There were a few moments of silence before Eiko had a question. "Hana, have you always lived in Sapporo?"

"No. My family only came here about three years ago, when my Father was transferred because of work. I think, in two more years, we will be moving back to Kobe."

"Have you liked Sapporo? It is definitely difficult during the winter months, when snow can fall from October through May. It is not just *samui*, cold, but *shibireru*, extremely cold."

Hana offered a slight smile. "We will probably get used to it about the time we move back to Honshu Island." She chuckled.

"Have you gone to the annual Sapporo Snow Festival?" Eiko asked. "As you probably know, it is so beautiful that a million or more tourists come from all over Japan and around the world to see it. It is always scheduled for the first part of February and lasts about a week. It is coming up soon, although I think I will have to watch it on television this year because of my leg. I want to get back to Tokyo as soon as I can. It is too great a risk to slip on some ice and injure myself again."

"My family usually watches it on TV, too," Hana answered. "But I will suggest we go to see it up close this year. Then, when we return to Kobe, we will have something awesome to share about Hokkaido."

Hana paused then, her expression wistful. "I so appreciate your kindness when I had trouble sleeping. I was lonely when my mom had to leave. This is my first time to be hospitalized."

Eiko nodded. "It is my first time, too. I understand. It is not easy being put in this environment."

"You mentioned Jesus. You said Jesus was my Friend, and He would always be with me and never leave. I have not heard about Jesus before. Who is He?"

Eiko thought her heart might burst with joy, as she responded to Hana's obviously heartfelt question. "Jesus is Almighty God's one and only Son. God sent Him to earth to teach us about God's love for us."

Hana appeared to be listening intently, so Eiko continued with her explanation. "Jesus lived a perfect life but willingly died on the Cross to make payment for everyone's wrongdoing. After three days, He rose from the grave. He is a living Savior, who desires people everywhere to be in a relationship with Him."

She smiled at Hana's rapt attention. "God's amazing grace and free gift of salvation are for all who follow Him. He even prepares a place for us, called heaven, where we can live with Him forever."

"He did all that for everyone? For me? This is the first time I have ever heard this."

Eiko nodded. "Have you heard about the Bible? It is God's love letter to us. It tells us all about His love and the way He works in people's lives. It is read all over the world, in many languages."

Eiko saw tears glistening in Hana's eyes. "Thank you for telling me about Jesus and the Bible. Maybe I can get a Bible someday and read how much God loves me."

Eiko looked at her New Testament on the bed stand, taking into consideration that, due to God's miraculous ways, she now had her papa's Bible to read. She picked up the New Testament and got out of her bed to hand it to Hana. "Here. I want you to have this. This is my first Bible. I got it when I attended a Christian woman's wake at a church. Everyone who attended received one. I have been reading this Bible regularly, but now that I have another one, I will not be needing this one."

Hana received the book and flipped through it, then she looked up at Eiko and asked, "What does it mean when certain places are underlined?"

Eiko smiled. "Oh, I did that because those verses are special to me, and I wanted to be able to find them again. As you read, you might want to do the same thing, in a different color of ink, so you can spot yours right away. You can start now if you like. I will give you some privacy."

The door opened then, and a nurse wheeled another patient into their room. She was placed across from Hana, in the first bed on the other side of the room. Eiko took the opportunity, while the new patient settled in, to rest on her bed for a little while, with her privacy curtain pulled. Yu had told her he was not coming for a visit today, so he could have a special talk with Mother about Papa's faith.

Eiko was overwhelmed that her sweet papa had never told her about Jesus while he was alive. It was such a disappointment to her. She prayed and asked the Lord to help her deal with the sudden news that Papa had been a Christian. If only the family had known this before his wake and funeral, her father's service would have been a Christian one, rather than Buddhist.

Eiko remembered the Christian wake at a church in Tokyo, which she attended with her friend Satoh, when her employer's wife, Mrs. Itoh, passed away. The service had singing and words full of hope, all of which the Buddhist ceremony was lacking. Eiko soon drifted off to sleep, as she once again mourned her father's death.

She awoke when she heard unrecognizable voices in the room. Directly across from her bed, she saw another patient getting settled in, meaning that the room would now be full. This patient was quite elderly, and several members of her family were talking with the nurses about her care. Next to this patient and across from Hana, was the middle-aged woman, who had come in this morning. As Eiko took stock of her new roommates, she decided to take a walk before dinner. She remembered to grab the pre-paid phone card the Sakamotos had sent her in the mail, so she could make some calls on the public phone in the visitor area.

Eiko stepped out gingerly and at a slow pace without her crutches. She knew she needed more practice, as she was still favoring her injured, but healing, left leg. And yet, she had to admit her physical therapy was helping to reduce her limp to minimal. She still had ten days before she was scheduled to be discharged, and she hoped to see even more progress by then. Overall, Eiko was pleased with the results and gave praise to the Lord for His mercy in her time of need.

As she entered the visitors' lounge, Eiko was surprised to find it much less crowded than she had expected it to be on a Sunday. She inserted the card in the phone and dialed the Sakamotos' number. It rang several times, and then she heard the voice of their oldest son, Ichiro, say, "Moshi moshi." Eiko spoke with Ichiro for a few minutes, until he passed the phone to his younger brother, Daisuke, so Ichiro could go get their father, who was downstairs at the fish market. The boys had said their mother was in Yokohama for the day, visiting her sister.

After speaking with Daisuke for a few moments, Mr. Sakamoto came on the line. "Moshi moshi, Eiko san. Ogenki desuka, how are you?"

"Goshimpai naku, Mr. Sakamoto. My leg is healing well, and I hope to return to Tokyo in a month. I miss everyone. It is great to hear your happy voice."

"*Onaji desu.* I am the same as you. It is nostalgic to hear your voice as well. Our family cannot wait until you once again join us at our table for dinner."

"I look forward to that, too. Well, I will keep this short so I can call again. Take care, my friend."

"You, too, Eiko san. Odaiji ni, take care of your health. Goodbye."

"I will. Goodbye."

Eiko inserted the card into the phone once again and called Sayuri, but no one answered. She imagined she was probably still at church for an afternoon activity with the young career group. Eiko loved being part of the group and was sad she couldn't be there with them. She remembered the many greeting cards she recently received from so many of her church friends, and it made her longing to see them that much more intense.

The phone went to the answering machine then, so Eiko left a brief message. "Sayuri, this is Eiko. Arigatou for all the cards. I loved them. It was so kind of all of you. My leg is healing, and I cannot wait to return to Tokyo and see you all again. Arigatou for your many prayers. God is answering. Bye, bye."

Eiko took out the phone card and put it in her pocket, ready to return to her room. She was hungry and hoped there would be something good for dinner.

When she got back, there were still a lot of visitors in the room. She decided to take out her papa's Bible and read some more in Psalms and Proverbs, while she waited for dinner to arrive.

Eiko started where she left off the day before, in Psalm 30. The words in verse 2 grabbed her heart as she read them: "Lord, my God, I prayed to you, and you healed me." Eiko was convinced the Lord would continue the healing in her leg, until it worked perfectly again. She made a promise to herself that she would always remember God's kindness each time she saw her scars. Eiko also believed God used the surgeon and nurses to be part of her healing miracle.

In verse 19 of Psalm 31, Eiko discovered this meaningful verse: "How great is your goodness that you have stored up for those who fear you, that you have given to those who trust you. You do this for all to see." In silent meditation, Eiko offered up a prayer. *I thank You, Lord Jesus, for taking all of my bad and giving me all of Your good, when You died on the Cross for me. It was an unfair trade for You, but the Bible says it was Your plan, from the very beginning, to save and redeem all of humanity. Thank You for Your goodness. I do not deserve it, but as Your child, I receive it because You are a loving Father. Thank You.*

Eiko teared up as she read from Psalm 34, verse 18: "The LORD is near to those who are discouraged; he saves those who have lost all hope." Eiko wiped the tears from her eyes, glad her privacy curtain was closed. She was also thankful that her bed was by the window because she enjoyed the majestic view of the snow-capped mountains outside. Eiko realized how much she missed seeing the amazing natural beauty in Hokkaido's four seasons while living on her own in Tokyo, nicknamed "the concrete city." From her apartment in Tokyo, she couldn't see a sunrise or sunset because of the tall buildings that blocked her view.

Eiko had not experienced any real crushing blows to her heart as she grew up. For the most part, life had been pleasant for her. Now, having experienced Papa's death, she knew what pain and brokenness felt like. To hear that God is close to those who are discouraged and have lost their hope was overwhelming to her.

Even though Eiko had now experienced feeling crushed by her circumstances, she knew God was there with her. He orchestrated events and people in her life to ease that pain. *I know my best Friend, Jesus, never left me alone,* she thought. *He was always with me. Always caring, always loving me through each new day, as He is now.*

Dinner came, and she was surprised to see that it was *oyakodon,* from "oya," meaning parent, "ko," meaning child, and "don," meaning a meal that is served over rice in a bowl. She loved oyakodon, a Japanese dish of sauteed chicken and cooked egg in a sauce, poured over rice. She hadn't had it in a while, and it was one of her favorite dishes. She was thankful her meal plan was no longer so strict, as it had been earlier in her recovery. She glanced around the room and noticed that everyone had received the same meal, except for the elderly woman across from her. Perhaps she had other health issues, Eiko thought. The dessert for Eiko and the others was another mikan, a sweet, juicy fruit she never tired of eating. Her mouth watered as she looked at her food with appreciation, before whispering a prayer of thanks and digging in.

After the dinner trays were picked up by the hospital workers, Eiko once again took out her father's Bible. She wanted to read a few more psalms before she turned out her light. She began reading in verse 7 of Psalm 37: "Be patient and wait for the LORD to act." Eiko thought about the wisdom of waiting on God. She knew He was capable of meeting our deepest needs at the most strategic moments of our lives.

It is definitely not easy for me to wait patiently for anything, she told herself. *In fact, it is uncomfortable to do so, especially because I love doing things my way. But the way God cared for me as I moved to Tokyo, while searching for meaning in life, and how He cared for me when my papa died, and how He is, even now, restoring my health and giving me hope for better days ahead, makes me willing to wait on Him every time.*

She closed her eyes. *You know how it is for me to be still before You, Lord. But as I read Your Word and pray, I can be silent in thought, trying to comprehend how Jesus Christ, the One and only Son of Almighty God, wants to be my personal Friend.*

Monday through Friday passed quickly, with several sessions of physical therapy and more walking practice in the hallways. Eiko got a positive report from her physical therapist, who was pleased with her latest progress. She was encouraged by the good news, knowing she was just days away from leaving the hospital.

Several other notable things happened during the week. Etsuko was not able to visit because she had gotten the flu. With the extra time she had without her mother's visits, Eiko had written several letters on the stationery her first roommate insisted she leave with her when she was allowed to go home. Eiko wrote a letter to Hope Tanner in America, as well as letters to her church friends in Tokyo. She also wrote a letter to her employer, thanking him for holding her job for her until she returned. Eiko shared with him that her recovery at the hospital was coming to a close, but her doctor wanted her to stay in town three more weeks at her family home to finish some physical therapy outpatient appointments.

Eiko tried to be helpful to her roommates. She often checked on the elderly woman, who was not able to get out of bed because of her broken hip. Occasionally, when her family member stepped out for a break, Eiko offered to fluff her pillow or pour more water in her pitcher. The woman didn't speak much but managed a slight smile to show her appreciation. Eiko also prayed silently for her that the Lord would do for this woman everything He had done for her.

The middle-aged woman by the door had been in a lot of pain. She'd had back surgery and was in a brace, which made it impossible for her to move about. Her older sister came to take care of her every day, and Eiko sat with her occasionally before her sister arrived in the afternoon. It was during those times she noticed the woman had a statue of Buddha on her bed stand. As Eiko sat quietly praying for this very private lady, Jesus helped her to be a sweet blessing to the woman in her pain.

Eiko looked forward to seeing her brother the next day. Since the beds in the room were filled with patients and the room with visitors, she knew it would seem a little crowded for Yu's taste. So when he arrived on Saturday, she decided she would walk with him to the visitors' area and spend time with him there. Saturday and Sunday would be Yu's final visits. By the following weekend, she would already be home with Mother, Yu, and her precious Kiku. She missed her Siamese cat so much, and she was convinced Kiku missed her, too.

Eiko spent a lot of time wondering how her last three weeks at home would be. Would there be opportunities to have meaningful conversations with her mother? Would she be able to have some fun times before she left for Tokyo? Would the remaining therapy outpatient appointments be difficult for her to complete?

She reminded herself of the need to put everything in the Lord's hands. She knew He would help her final weeks happen the way He intended. All she needed to do was wait on His timing and trust in His good plans for her.

CHAPTER NINE

The winter morning dawned a beautiful nihonbare, sky blue. Eiko was up early and walked down the hallway to use the restroom and take a shower. When she was done, she put on her clean Ling-Ling giant panda pajamas and her robe, rejoicing as she walked that her left leg felt stronger each day.

Coming back to her room, she greeted her roommates, who were all awake. "Ohayou gozaimasu!"

Hana, right by the door, answered back. "Ohayou gozaimasu."

"It is a beautiful day that the Lord has made," Eiko declared, then began humming the melody that accompanied those words in a worship song, taken straight from the Scriptures. It was a happy song, and it came to her mind often, since learning it at the church retreat in the mountains. The scenery there had reminded Eiko of the majestic beauty of Hokkaido. She remembered one morning at the retreat, when she arose early and hiked up the mountain behind the retreat center. As she overlooked the little valley below, she was treated to the most awesome sunrise. That was the moment she remembered as the first time she thanked Creator God for His beautiful creation all around her.

After breakfast, Eiko asked Hana if she would like to go for a walk with her. Hana quickly agreed, and the two of them strolled down the nearly deserted hallway. Eiko had been at the hospital long enough to know that things were fairly quiet on Saturdays, so it was no surprise that they had the corridor nearly to themselves.

The two young women went to the visitors' lounge and sat down for a few minutes. "Nihonbare," Hana commented, as she looked out the window. "Those are my favorite days."

"Mine, too," Eiko declared with a smile. "But I have been learning lately that I appreciate the cloudless, bright sky blue even more after periods of endless clouds gray. When the clouds are gray, we know a storm is coming. Those storms can last for days or sometimes weeks. But when they have finally passed, the bright sky blue returns faithfully. It makes me feel hopeful that the future is going to be bright, too, no matter how many storms I face in my lifetime."

When Hana didn't respond, Eiko went on. "I understand now that storms can be blessings. Our earth is blessed, as it receives its much needed rain, which makes everything green and alive, like a bamboo forest. I have been meditating on the need to accept each day as a gift from God and to trust Him for what happens in my life. He wants to bless each of us, through both storms and perfect-weather days, just because He loves us so much."

Hana nodded but still didn't speak, so Eiko concluded that her roommate had heard her words and that God would work them out in her heart in His time.

Yu came in the afternoon and was happy to visit with Eiko in the visitors' lounge. Once they'd found seats, he opened a small bag and handed it to her. "Thought you might like this."

Eiko looked inside and saw her favorite chocolate-covered almonds. "Thanks, big brother, for spoiling me. You and Mother know how much I love these."

"I do. By the way, Mother says 'hi.'"

"How is she doing?"

"She is improving...slowly. I am not sure she will be able to see you here at the hospital before you make it home on Wednesday. She is still pretty weak."

Eiko drew her brows together, concerned. "Is it the flu that is going around, or is it something more?"

"Well, I think something else might be bothering her a bit," Yu admitted. "You remember last week? I did not come to visit on Sunday because I wanted to talk with Mother."

Eiko nodded. "You were going to ask her about Papa being a Christian. I have been praying all week that the truth would come out. What did she say? I am eager to learn more."

"It turns out that Mother discovered, on her own, what was in the package that Uncle Yoshi's best friend left for you when he visited Sapporo. The part about Kiku scratching and making holes in the wrapping paper was only partly the truth. Mother was curious, so she opened it and found Papa's Bible. Afterwards, she re-wrapped it and removed it from your room, hoping you would not remember to ask about it."

Eiko's heart skipped a beat. "Mother was wrong, thinking I would give up on finding it. I wonder why she changed her mind and had you bring it to me when you visited last Saturday."

"I think she felt guilty. She cried several times, while telling me about Father becoming a Christian. It turns out that before they were married, he told her about his decision to trust in Jesus Christ and that he had been baptized in his freshman year of college. Father begged Mother to support the decision he had made years before they met. He also begged her to attend church with him, to learn how much God loved her. She admitted she was stubborn and refused. When she told her parents, they added fuel to the fire. With them backing her, she stayed firm in her decision to remain a Buddhist, even if it cost her the loss of her future husband."

"Poor Papa." Tears stung Eiko's eyes, but she blinked them back. She would make them wait until she was alone. "How very sad for both of them." *Please, Lord, I do not want that to happen to me. I do not want to marry someone who does not support or share my faith in You, Almighty God. I want my husband to know Your love for him, too. I want to have a Christian marriage, like Aki and Yoko in Yokohama. Their marriage relationship is filled with faith, hope, and love because You are their foundation.*

Yu interrupted her thoughts. "Mother said Father was so disappointed that he almost called off the wedding but, in the end, he could not. He was so in love with Mother that he could not give her up at that point. They married and had us in the early years. And as you know, they loved us and faithfully provided for us as we grew up."

"Yes," Eiko agreed. "It seems Papa did not hold a grudge at all. He was always in a good mood, and his words were soft-spoken. I miss him so much. You do, too, right?"

Yu nodded, his dark hair shining in the overhead light. "I do miss him, Eiko. But now we have a mother who needs our love and acceptance, and we need to help her, like Father would if he were still alive." Yu looked around the visitors' lounge before continuing. They had the place to themselves. "Mother believes God is punishing her now because, years ago, she refused to allow Christ into their home."

Eiko laid a hand on Yu's. "God would not do that, Yu. He loves everyone the same. His forgiveness and His free gift of salvation are available to every person. Mother can experience God's amazing love, just like Papa and I did when we decided to believe that Almighty God is the One true God, and there is no other. We believe God sent His one and only Son, Jesus Christ, to the earth to show us how much God wants us to be in a right relationship with Him."

Yu seemed thoughtful. "Mother did not have an opportunity to learn the truth, like Father did."

"She did when Papa shared with her what Jesus meant to him."

"But she did not have any experience going to church. Neither did her parents, before they passed away."

Eiko heard the hopelessness in her brother's voice. "How do you know that? How do I know that for sure? Maybe Almighty God reached out to Mother's parents at some point, and to Mother too, even before meeting Papa."

She leaned closer, as her intensity increased. "I only found out about God because Sayuri at work told me about Him. I thought it was my first time to hear about Almighty God, but then God helped me remember my friend in elementary school, who was a Christian. I remember my classmates would not include her in their activities. I talked with her sometimes and found her to be very kind."

When Yu shrugged, she continued. "My classmate talked about church sometimes, but it all sounded strange to me at that age. I think her father was a pastor. Her joyful spirit was proof that she had a loving Savior as her best Friend. She did not react when the kids were mean to her. God helped her rise above it. Even at her young age, she was courageous. If she could be that courageous in her faith at her age, I know I can be even braver at mine."

Yu's nod was nearly imperceptible, but it was enough that Eiko was encouraged when he said, "I guess that makes sense." Yu ran his hand through his hair, giving it a tousled look. "I am thirsty, Eiko. How about you? I think I will go to the basement cafeteria and get us both something to drink. What would you like?"

"I would love a cup of hot cocoa, please—if they have it."

"Why don't I meet you back in your room?" Yu suggested. "You should probably put your leg up for a while."

When Yu was gone, Eiko returned to her room and was soon glad that her leg now rested on the bed. The chairs in the visitors' lounge were not very comfortable.

In minutes, Yu walked in with her hot chocolate and a coffee for himself. She offered her brother some of her chocolate-covered almonds.

"Thanks," he said, popping a few in his mouth. "I think I will." As he sat down in the chair by her bed, he grinned. "These are good."

Eiko nodded, then asked about Yu's work situation. He shared with her that it was somewhat better. They talked about the total snowfall in January and the difficulty of keeping the driveway and sidewalk area cleared in front of their home. "I cannot wait to get you out of the hospital so you can help me."

Eiko looked at Yu to see if he was teasing, and she could tell he was struggling to keep a straight face. "So how is Kiku?" she asked, changing the subject.

Yu's smile broke out then. "Oh, Kiku is Kiku—always interested in what everyone around her is doing. The other day, she was lying too close to the fireplace, when an ember fell on her tail. She cried and ran to Mother's lap. Mother said she did not think Kiku caught an ember. She believes Kiku's only purpose was to get some sympathy and to hear some comforting words. Later, we could not find her. We looked in lots of places and finally found her sleeping soundly on your bed. Perhaps she was looking for more sympathy, but you were not there."

Eiko sighed. "I cannot wait to get home. The time in the hospital has passed slowly."

"My boss is letting me have Wednesday off next week to bring you home from the hospital," Yu announced.

Eiko was pleased. "That is nice of him."

"Well, not as nice as you might think." Yu grinned. "I have to work that Saturday to make up for the missed day."

Eiko smiled. "Thanks for doing that for me. You are a sweet brother. God loves you, and so do I."

Yu lifted his eyebrows. "Okay, this conversation is getting too mushy for me, so I am going to head home now. I will come by tomorrow afternoon."

"Would you please bring our portable chess game?" Eiko grinned. "We have not played in a long time, and I need a challenge. How about it?"

Yu shrugged. "Sure, if you are certain you are up to it." He chuckled and walked away before she could answer.

He is a great chess player, Eiko thought , *but occasionally I win. I hope that happens tomorrow.*

Monday morning, during her physical therapy, Eiko thought about her Sunday win at chess. She had teased Yu about his loss, and he responded by teasing her that she just got lucky.

"How is it feeling now?" the therapist, Tanaka san, asked, interrupting her thoughts.

"It feels better," she admitted, "now that the outer stitches have been removed and the surgical scars are healing."

Tanaka san smiled. "Great. We have just one last session tomorrow. Then, during the three weeks you are home, the doctor wants you to see me a total of six more times. After that, he will give you a note for your employer, saying you are cleared to work."

Eiko stood and smiled. "I am so ready to go back to work."

"I am sure you are," he agreed.

Eiko left the room, feeling as if she were floating on air.

Eiko could scarcely sit still, as she awaited Yuitsu's arrival at the hospital Wednesday morning. By the time he walked into the room, both Eiko and her overnight bag were packed and ready to go.

Yu grinned. "Are you sure you do not want to stay a few more days?"

Eiko chuckled. "Very funny, Brother."

In minutes, the nurses had come in, bringing the forms that needed to be signed before she could leave. Once those were done, Yu left to take Eiko's things out to the car, before coming back to get her. Eiko used that time to say goodbye to her roommates, encouraging them that she was praying for their healing so they, too, could return home soon.

Eiko stepped out of the hospital room that had been her home for five weeks, just as Yu got off the elevator on the third floor, the last time he would do so after many visits to see Eiko. She was pleased at the look of admiration on his face, as he watched her walk to the elevator, her steps flowing so smoothly that she imagined it was difficult to know by sight which leg had been injured.

When they got off the elevator on the main floor, a wheelchair waited for her at the front counter. Although she didn't like it, she understood that it was hospital policy, and so she allowed the nurse to push her to the closest access point to Yu's car. Eiko and Yu then walked together to where the car was parked. Eiko had tears in her eyes, as she rejoiced in her new freedom to be outside, walking on her own.

Yu held on to her as he helped her into the car. Eiko's excitement grew, as they drove to their home and went inside to greet Mother. Etsuko met them at the door, all smiles, as she told them lunch was ready. Yu went back out to get Eiko's things, then ran them upstairs to her room, even as Kiku rubbed against Eiko's legs and purred ever so sweetly. Eiko reached down to pick her up and stroke her soft fur.

As they went into the kitchen to sit down at the table, Eiko noticed their favorite local restaurant had delivered ramen and *gyouza*, which Etsuko had ordered special for them.

Eiko put Kiku down, washed her hands in the sink, and hugged Mother. "Thank you for the special treat, Mom. As you know, I love ramen here in Hokkaido more than in Tokyo. And an order of gyouza is perfect with a bowl of ramen."

Then, surprisingly, Mother asked Eiko to say a prayer before the meal. Eiko was happy to do so, though she couldn't help but wonder what was going on in Mother's mind.

"Loving God," Eiko began, "thank You for Mother and Yu's help while I had a broken leg. Thank You for giving them to me. We all thank You for this delicious meal we can share together. In Jesus' name, I pray. Amen."

Soon they were happily slurping their ramen and enjoying their time together. By the time the meal was over, not even one of the gyouza was left. Mother got up and poured everyone a cup of ocha, a relaxing ending after a delicious and satisfying meal.

"I have a fire going in the living room," Etsuko said." Let us go enjoy it. We can take another cup of ocha with us."

Yu picked up the ramen bowls and gyouza plates and rinsed them at the sink. Then he placed them outside the door so the man on the scooter could pick them up and return them to the restaurant.

When he was finished, all three of them went into the living room and sat down on the sofa, where they could watch the logs, blazing in the fireplace. Kiku immediately jumped up on Eiko's lap and was soon fast asleep.

As Kiku snoozed, the three of them caught up on some of the neighborhood talk and family news that had taken place while Eiko was in the hospital. Mother said some mail had come for Eiko, which she had set aside for her. She went to retrieve it and handed it to her daughter.

Among the offering was a small package from Sayuri. Eiko opened it first and discovered a painting that her friend had promised to send her. It showed the mountain retreat where they had gone with the young adults from church. Eiko showed it to Yu and Mother, and told them her friend had painted it.

"It is lovely, dear," Mother said, closely examining the fine details of the amber, orange, and red autumn leaves, with different shapes, according to the tree.

"It looks professional," Yu added. "Sayuri must have been painting all of her life."

"Actually, this is her first painting in many years," Eiko explained. "I hope this is the beginning of a career, where she can sell her paintings."

Eiko set the painting aside and found a letter from the Sakamoto family. They told her some of the things going on at the fish market, and they also reported that they had been getting her mail from the mailbox and putting it inside her genkan every couple of days. Eiko was happy to read that her houseplants were thriving.

Eiko passed the Sakamotos' letter to her Mom and Yu to read, while she opened a letter from her employer. Mr. Itoh said Eiko's coworkers at the company were looking forward to her return. She passed that on to her family to read, also.

The last envelope contained a letter from Satoh. She decided not to pass that around, as she wanted privacy concerning her special friend. She wasn't sure what her heart felt about him, but she knew she felt comfortable being around him—most of the time. On occasion, he would get his feelings hurt and walk away, and that is what concerned her the most. *One good thing,* she reminded herself, *is that Satoh is open to going to church with me. I love that about him.*

Eiko decided to pray and ask the Lord what she should do about Satoh. He had given her that beautiful necklace, but she didn't want to deceive him by wearing it if her heart wasn't right.

Eiko open his letter and braced herself for whatever it contained.

Chapter Ten

*E*iko, the letter began, *I hope you will understand what I need to ask you. I have been pleased with how well your recovery is going, but I worry about your trip home, without anyone to help you. For example, it might not be good for you to carry a heavy bag, even though your leg has healed. So I would like to fly to Sapporo and travel home with you to Tokyo. Would you allow me that privilege? I am ready to purchase my tickets as soon as I get your blessing. I cannot wait to see you again. I have missed you.*

Eiko tucked Satoh's letter back in its envelope, excused herself, gently moved Kiku from her lap, then headed upstairs to her bedroom, treating her leg carefully as she climbed the stairs. She unpacked her overnight bag and put her papa's Bible on her bed. She then turned to the Psalms and continued reading where she had left off. When she was finished, she put the bookmark in place and closed the Bible.

How special it was to hold the Bible that her sweet papa had held in his hands in college! She prayed for several minutes before going back downstairs. Eiko decided to ask Yu and Mother what they thought about Satoh coming to Sapporo to travel home to Tokyo with her. Eiko knew he would need at least a week to be able to get the best price. In all fairness, he needed to hear from her in the next few days.

She found her mother and brother still in the living room. Yu was reading the financial pages in the newspaper, while Etsuko read a Japanese novel by a Hokkaido author, also known for her Christian faith.

Kiku had relocated on Etsuko's lap, but she immediately hopped off and came to Eiko. Not wanting to interrupt her mother or brother, Eiko sat down on the sofa and played with Kiku, who seemed to want Eiko to bat around her toy mouse.

After a few minutes, the phone rang, and Eiko went to answer it. "Moshi moshi."

"Moshi moshi. May I please speak to Eiko san? This is Mari, her friend."

Eiko smiled. It was good to speak with Hope's friend, who had now become her friend, as well. "Hi, Mari san. This is Eiko. Mother told me you called while I was in hospital."

"Yes," Mari replied. "I was so sad to hear about your skiing accident. How is your recovery going?"

"It is going well. I know God has been watching over me. The doctor says I can return to Tokyo in three weeks. I am so excited!"

She could almost hear Mari's smile through the phone. "That is great, Eiko san. Would it be okay if I came by to visit you this week?"

"Sure! I would like that."

"Okay, thanks. Last week, Hope called from America and said she wanted to get you a baptism gift from the small Christian bookstore in town. I wanted to go in on it, too, so I will be going to the store this week and will bring it by when I come."

"That is sweet of you, Mari san—and of Hope, too. Thank you."

"It is something we want to do. I will call first before I come, to make sure it is a good time for you."

"Arigatou, Mari san."

"Goodbye."

"Bye, bye."

When Eiko rejoined her family on the couch, Etsuko asked if she had enjoyed talking with Mari san.

Eiko nodded. "Yes. She is really nice." She hesitated, then decided to forge ahead. "I have been wanting to talk with you about another friend. You may remember that I have mentioned Satoh kun several times in our phone calls. He is a coworker and a friend in Tokyo, whom I have spent some time with outside of the office." Looking over at Yu until he raised his head up from the newspaper, she continued. "I also want my big brother to be in on this conversation. Okay?"

"I am listening," Yu responded. "Please, go on."

She took a deep breath. "I want to tell you about the letter I received today from Satoh kun."

Yu grinned and removed his glasses. "I thought you shared all of your mail with us earlier. This guy must be pretty special."

"What is it, dear?" Etsuko asked.

"Satoh is worried about me traveling home to Tokyo by myself," she explained. "My leg is strong, and my walking is good, but he worries that I should not be carrying a heavy bag around. He wants to come to Sapporo and make the return trip to Tokyo with me, to help me out if I need it. I just want to know what you both think. Does that seem strange?"

"I would say he is in love with you, Eiko," Yu commented.

Mother added, "He does sound like he cares for you very much. Does that worry you? Do you care for him?"

"I am not sure about my feelings," Eiko admitted. "Now that I am a Christian, I want to fall in love with a Christian man so we can have the same faith."

A cloud passed over Etsuko's face, and for a moment, she ducked her head. Instantly, Eiko identified the problem. "Oh, Mother. I am so sorry. I am not judging you. In fact, our hearts are similar because you were Buddhist and wanted to marry a Buddhist for harmony in your home. I feel the same way." Eiko was relieved when her mother lifted her head. "Satoh is really a nice guy," she went on, "but he does not want to be a Christian. Yet he is willing to go to church with me sometimes. I know that is a positive thing. I just do not want to compromise my dream of having a Christian husband, who loves the Lord and serves Him."

"Flying to Tokyo with you does not mean you are walking down the aisle of a church to get married," Yu said.

"Maybe Satoh kun's idea came from the God you love," Mother suggested with a soft voice.

"Yes, maybe so." Surprised by her mother's comment, Eiko was somehow hesitant.

Etsuko's eyes narrowed as she focused on Eiko's face. "Do you believe God loves me, Eiko?"

Eiko caught her breath. "Yes. I know that for sure, Mom. He loves everyone and everything that He created. We do not have to do anything special to be loved by God. But we have to do something special to be in a right relationship with a loving and holy God. We have to trust in Him as a loving Creator and believe He has created a wonderful plan for each of our lives. We need to receive His forgiveness for our wrongdoings, as we receive His free gift of salvation. Salvation comes through Jesus, God's one and only Son, who died on the Cross, was buried, and rose again on the third day. He lives inside us and will never leave us or forsake us. He promises us an eternal home with Him—forever in heaven."

Doubt danced across Etsuko's face. "So your father believed all that—and he did that? And did God accept him, even though he received a Buddhist wake and funeral?"

Eiko answered carefully, knowing Yu listened intently to see how she would respond. "Mom, I believe Papa is in heaven with Jesus right now. If he was not there, I do not think we would be having this conversation right now. Do you remember when Papa opened his eyes that day in the hospital? It was when I was telling him about how I wanted to know more about Jesus, after Sayuri told me about His love for me."

Mother nodded, no doubt remembering how upset her daughter had been when her papa's eyes closed again, and the doctor told her that sometimes that happens to patients in comas. Eiko had hoped it meant he was trying to wake up to speak to her.

"Well, I now believe Papa was trying to encourage me to follow Jesus," Eiko said. "You remember how I got my job in Tokyo before I moved there, right? It was Uncle Yoshi's best friend in college, whose relative owns the company. Uncle Yoshi's friend, Watanabe san, was also a friend of Papa's through the years, after Uncle Yoshi died. Perhaps Papa called this friend, who we found out recently is a Christian, and he recommended his relative's business in Tokyo. This family friend, Mr. Watanabe, said in his letter to me that he has been praying for our family for years. I believe he is the one who helped me get work in Tokyo, and Tokyo is the place where I heard the Good News about Jesus for the first time. God used him to get me there, with Papa's help."

"I think you are taking that a little too far, Eiko," Yu said. "It just might be a coincidence."

Mother chimed in then. "I remember your father telling me he knew just the right friend to help Eiko. That makes me believe it was intentional."

"And do not forget that Watanabe san said he knew God wanted me to have Papa's Bible, so he brought it with him on his vacation to Hokkaido and left it at the house for me. God knew it would mean so much to me to read from Papa's first Bible, the one he used in his college days. It is a miracle, I believe, which God had planned long before I was born."

Yu changed the subject. "Well, back to Satoh kun. I say, invite him to come up to Sapporo on Friday after work. He can stay in my room on Friday and Saturday nights before you leave late Sunday afternoon for Tokyo."

Yu's eyes took on an amused sparkle. "Did you not tell me he teases you about how much you love Hokkaido ramen? We should plan to take him out to our favorite ramen shop while he is here. Maybe he will change his mind about Tokyo ramen being his favorite."

Eiko's excitement was building. "And I would love to take Satoh kun to the church I visited the first Sunday I was back in Sapporo. It is full of young people, just starting out in their careers. They have a band that plays the praise music, and the preaching was interesting, too. It is different from my church in Tokyo, which I love very much. But this church is also nice because it focuses on the younger generation's needs. Yu, would you like to attend with Satoh kun and me?"

Yu paused before answering. "I will think about it. I am not making any promises."

Eiko thanked both of them for helping her to think through her decision to invite Satoh kun to Sapporo. Now she knew what she would say when she called him in the morning.

Eiko went over to her mom and gave her a hug before going into the kitchen to heat up some leftovers for dinner.

Two and a half weeks later, Eiko began packing for her return trip to Tokyo. Since Satoh was coming to help Eiko, she decided to take a larger suitcase so she could include some of her spring clothes, which she had left behind when she moved. She also made room to take Sayuri's small painting to hang in her apartment, and a gift from Hope and Mari to use in her kitchen.

True to her word, Mari had brought by a beautiful white porcelain teacup and saucer, showing purple grape clusters hanging from a strong vine. It reminded Eiko of Sayuri's *obentou* cover that she used to carry her lunch to work. It had the same design, and Eiko had thought it quite lovely the first time she saw it. She had recently learned that the design was a favorite of Christians because of a popular Bible verse, where Jesus said in John 15:5, "I am the vine, and you are the branches. Those who remain in me, and I in them, will bear much fruit; for you can do nothing without me." Eiko cherished the teacup and her friendship with Hope and Mari, which she was confident would continue in the future.

Eiko was proud that she had successfully finished her six appointments of outpatient physical therapy and received a note from her surgeon, saying that her leg was healed and she could go back to work right away after returning to Tokyo.

She closed up her suitcase and set it on the floor. She also had a small denim bag, which she used to put her Bible in, so she could carry it with her on the plane. She wanted to keep it close to her always. *I will never forget what You have done for me, Lord, and for my family. I am forever grateful.*

In about an hour, Eiko and Yu would be on their way to Chitose airport to pick up Satoh kun. Eiko hoped her mother and brother would like Satoh and get along well with him. Yu had already put down a nice futon and cover in his room for Satoh to sleep on. Yu and Satoh were going to use the guest bathroom, while Eiko would use the bathroom in Mother's room. Eiko was happy that Mother was preparing a special dinner for Satoh kun, of fish and vegetables, grown in Hokkaido. Eiko helped with the preparations by vacuuming Kiku's hair up in the living room, then she hurried upstairs to grab her leather purse.

Yu's voice called up the stairway, interrupting her thoughts. "Come on, Sis. It's time to go."

"Coming!" Before descending the stairs, Eiko put on the necklace Satoh kun had given her for Christmas.

The hour drive to the airport went well. Yu and Eiko then watched the restricted baggage area through the doors in front of them, waiting for the passengers to exit.

In a few minutes, Eiko spotted Satoh kun, coming down the steps, with a small bag slung over his shoulder. He came straight through the door, directly toward Eiko and Yu. When he drew up even with them, he reached out to shake Yu's hand before doing the same with Eiko. With a big smile on his face, he declared, "This is my first time in Hokkaido."

Yu grinned. "We hope you enjoy your stay."

The three of them walked out to the white mid-size Nissan and got in. Satoh started to get in the back seat, but Yu invited him to sit up front with him. On the way home, Satoh talked about his day at work and his flight to Sapporo. Occasionally he looked in the back seat and smiled at Eiko. She smiled back but remained quiet on the drive.

They arrived home, parked in the carport, and went inside to greet Mother. Satoh bowed to Etsuko and handed her a box of traditional buns, with sweet bean paste in the middle, from a well-known Tokyo bakery. Etsuko bowed in return and thanked him for the gift.

Yu then took Satoh up to his room for a few minutes before dinner, to show him where he would be sleeping. Eiko went into the kitchen to see if she could be of help.

Everything was ready by the time the guys came back downstairs. The cat seemed to be trying to make up her mind whether or not Satoh deserved to be greeted.

They all sat down at the table in the kitchen, with Satoh kun next to Eiko, while Mother and Yu sat across from them. "Eiko, would you like to say a prayer?" her mother asked.

Eiko bowed her head and thanked God for His provision and blessings and finished up by saying, "In Jesus' name I pray. Amen." After her amen, Yu and Mother said, "Itadakimasu," with Satoh joining in.

The meal was delicious, and Satoh asked if the ingredients were native to Hokkaido. Mother seemed pleased that he asked, and she continued to talk about all the wonderful foods one can buy in Hokkaido that can't be found elsewhere.

Yu asked for seconds, and so the serving dishes were passed around again. Afterward, Eiko got up to serve everyone some ocha. Finally, Mother asked Eiko to open the sweet buns and serve them with the green tea.

Eiko removed the dishes from the table, while the water boiled for the tea. When the table was clean, Eiko served the ocha and sweet buns. It was a nice ending to an excellent meal. She filled the teapot again for anyone who wanted a little more.

Mother then insisted she would do the dishes, shooing the others into the living room to enjoy the crackling fire. The three young adults argued that they could take care of the kitchen, but Etsuko wouldn't hear of it. Finally, the three gave in. Eiko sat down on the sofa, and Satoh took a seat beside her, while Yu sat in an adjacent chair. As they sat together, Satoh asked Eiko questions about life in Hokkaido.

Eiko was happy to answer his inquiries, and Yu waited quietly until they were finished, before he asked Satoh if he played chess.

Satoh smiled. "I do. I belonged to a chess club in high school."

"I did, too." Yu grinned, as he reached for the chess board on the bookshelf. He set up the game and asked Satoh to sit with him at the small chess table. Mother soon finished in the kitchen and came and sat by Eiko on the sofa. Kiku gave up on the men and decided to sit with the ladies, lying down between them and begging both of them to pet her. The feline's contented purring indicated she was enjoying every second of their attention.

Eiko watched the chess match and quickly decided that Yu and Satoh were evenly matched. They played two games in a row, with each winning one. They then decided to finish their competition the following day, as it was obvious everyone was tired and ready to go to bed.

In the morning, they had a simple breakfast with coffee. Later in the morning, Yu drove Satoh and Eiko around Sapporo to show their guest some famous spots. They went to Sheep Hill; Odori Park, where the Snow Festival takes place; the Sapporo TV Tower; the old Clock Tower building;

and ended up at the famous ramen shop in Sapporo, where the noodles were made from scratch each day, along with the fresh soup ingredients.

Satoh grinned. "Somehow I knew we would end up here."

Eiko laughed. "You have got to be convinced that Sapporo ramen is tastier than Tokyo ramen. I am sure you will notice the difference in the first mouthful."

When they sat down to try a bowl, it didn't take Satoh long to admit they were right. "The ramen is *oishii*, delicious!"

Eiko couldn't help but smile, pleased to have won Satoh over to her favorite ramen.

Back at home, Yu and Satoh set up the chess board and went back to playing. Eiko said she would play a game with the winner, and she suspected that Satoh tried extra hard to make sure he won. He did, and Eiko took Yu's place. She lost but graciously complimented Satoh.

Yu also complimented him. "Nice job, Satoh kun."

Eiko was pleased to see that Yu and Satoh seemed to be getting along so well.

By late evening, a storm had dumped quite a few inches of snow in the driveway. Yu excused himself to go shovel. Eiko and Satoh decided to help, though Satoh insisted Eiko take it easy. "You do not want to reinjure your leg," he reminded her.

She promised to be careful, and off they went. Three people shoveling got the job done much faster than Yu could have done on his own. Eiko worked on the narrow sidewalk to their front door, while the guys cleared out the driveway. Eiko finished first and then went inside to make some hot cocoa. It was ready when the guys came in.

Satoh thanked Eiko, as he held his steaming cup. "It is really cold out there. This is warming my hands and body. I love the natural taste, too."

Eiko then broached another topic with Satoh. "Do you remember me telling you about Mari chan's church, the one that has so many young people? I was hoping we could go tomorrow morning. What do you think?"

Satoh hesitated, but gave in quickly. "It sounds interesting. Yes. I want to go with you and check it out."

Eiko didn't even try to hide her happiness. Then she turned her attention to her brother. "Would you go with us, Yu?"

Again, she was met with hesitation, but again, it didn't last long. Yu agreed to come along.

For dinner Mother made *Ishikari nabe,* Hokkaido Salmon Hotpot, a delicious miso-based soup broth, with chunks of salmon and lots of vegetables, boiled in a pot on a gas burner on the table. Satoh seemed quite impressed and ate until he was full.

Before they knew it, another day had come to an end, and Eiko would soon be heading back to Tokyo at last.

Eiko's first thought upon waking was that it was her last day with her family—including the faithful Kiku, who now slept next to her on the bed. For just a moment, her heart twisted with melancholy, but then she thought of how exciting it would be to finally get back home to Tokyo and see all the wonderful friends she had made there.

She jumped out of bed and immediately began getting ready. About mid-morning, Yu, Satoh, and Eiko attended Mari chan's church. Eiko was pleased to be there again. She was especially happy that Satoh kun and Yu were with her. On their way home, Eiko asked them what they thought.

"I loved the music," Satoh confessed.

"I thought the preacher's message was interesting," Yu added.

"And the people were nice and friendly," Eiko said, "especially Mari chan. She was the one who came rushing over to greet us before she got up on the stage to sing the praise songs. Thanks for going with me, guys. It will stay in my memory for a long time."

After they returned home, Mother ordered some sushi from the local restaurant. When the food arrived, they all gathered around the kitchen table to eat their lunch. As they ate, the young people described to Etsuko what the church service was like. She said she wasn't sure she would like all of the noise, but Eiko assured her that there were other Christian churches in Sapporo, not all of them so exuberant or loud. Surely there would be one that would be a good match for her.

A thought popped into Eiko's mind then. "Do you have any friends that go to church, Mom?"

Etsuko nodded. "One of the ladies in our neighborhood goes to church. I am not sure where her church is. All of my good friends are Buddhist."

"Did you know any Christians when you were younger?" Eiko prodded.

"Actually, my parents sent me to a Christian *yochien*, a Japanese kindergarten. Some of the teachers were Christians, and some of the families, too."

"But your parents were Buddhist," Satoh observed. "Why did they send you to a Christian yochien?"

Mother seemed to be recalling, even as she spoke. "It had the best reputation in our town. Even though it cost money, there was always a long line of families trying to get their children into the school."

"Did you learn Bible verses and sing Christian songs?" Eiko asked.

129

"I did, but I have forgotten all of them." She smiled wistfully. "That was a long time ago. I was only four when I started."

"You know, Mother," Eiko said, "I think God chose you to learn about Him at a young age. It was a miracle of God's grace. Our family has been on God's heart from the very beginning."

Eiko glanced at Satoh and could see he was moved by the conversation. *Perhaps he is thinking about his own family. It is pretty amazing that Satoh's cousin Aki is the first Christian in his family.*

They all went into the living room then and turned on the TV. Ski-racing in Nagano was on, and they enjoyed watching the men's downhill competition and also the ladies' slalom. Before long, though, Mother commented that it was getting time to go to the airport. She got up to get ready and suggested everyone else do the same.

Eiko spent a few moments with Kiku, telling her precious cat that she and her friend Satoh had to go back to Tokyo today. Eiko promised she would be back to visit, and in the meantime, she hoped Kiku would be sweet to Mother and Yu.

About thirty minutes later, they put the suitcases in the trunk of the car. Mother rode up front with Yu, leaving Eiko and Satoh to sit in the back seat together. Fortunately, the weather had cleared, which made the drive very pleasant.

They pulled up to the curb at the airport departure area, then Mother and Yu got out to say goodbye. Yu got the suitcases out of the trunk and shook Satoh's hand. Mother hugged Eiko and bowed to Satoh.

"Thank you for taking Eiko back to Tokyo," she said.

"We will have to play chess again the next time we get together," Yu suggested.

Satoh agreed, as he picked up the bags and went into the airport with Eiko. They waved one more time from inside. Everything went smoothly at check-in and also at the security checkpoint. They soon boarded the plane, found their seats, and waited for take-off.

Satoh looked at Eiko. "I really enjoyed my weekend in Sapporo. You have a nice family; they treated me very kindly."

"I think they liked you a lot." She smiled. "That makes me happy."

"One thing I was not used to is the extreme cold," Satoh confessed. "I am ready to be back in Tokyo, even though shoveling snow was fun."

Eiko nodded. "I am ready to be back in Tokyo, too. I am happy with my life there."

Satoh's smile was warm. "I am glad to hear you say that. By the way, I noticed you have been wearing the heart necklace I gave you at Christmas."

Eiko felt her cheeks warm slightly, as she nodded. "It is really pretty. And I noticed you have been wearing the muffler I got you for Christmas. Did it help keep you warm while you were in Sapporo?"

"Yes, it did. I love it."

Satoh reached over and held her hand. Both of them closed their eyes for a few moments after the plane took off, lost in their own thoughts.

Before they knew it, the flight attendant got on the speaker to let the passengers know that the plane was on its final descent at Haneda airport and would be landing in ten minutes. The landing was smooth, and the passengers filed out of the plane rather quickly, since it wasn't a full flight.

Eiko and Satoh grabbed their luggage from the carousel and walked out to the lobby. They were prepared to ride the monorail and trains to get home, but they were surprised to see people they knew, waiting to greet them in the arrival lobby. They saw Sayuri, Mr. Itoh, Mr. Sakamoto, and several friends from church, all smiling at them. As Satoh and Eiko walked out to them, their friends cheered and welcomed Eiko home with a big bouquet of flowers.

"We missed you," they all said. Then Mr. Sakamoto said he had come by car, and Eiko and Satoh were to ride home with him.

Satoh kun thanked everyone for coming, then he asked Eiko chan if she wanted to say something.

She nodded and smiled. "May God be praised! He has healed my leg because of your prayers for me. I will always remember the love of Christ you have shown me. It is good to be back with all of you. I know He has special things planned for us, as we continue on our journey of faith together."

In a few moments, all who had gathered at the airport to welcome Eiko home were on their way to their individual homes, by train and by car, as Creator God Himself painted the most beautiful, majestic sunset of colors, illuminating the Tokyo sky as far as one can see.

My heart feels lighter
The clouds are disappearing
God's grace got me through.

Don't Miss the Other Books in the Sky Blue Trilogy!

Sky Blue: In 1993, with college graduation in Sapporo behind her, determined twenty-two-year-old Eiko sets her sights on living and working in the expansive metropolis of Tokyo. Her dream of exciting, new adventures in the big city gives her the strength and courage to leave behind all that she knows and loves—the familiarity and beauty of Hokkaido, her caring parents, her fun-loving older brother, and close friends—for the unknown in Tokyo.

Somewhat inexperienced, Eiko could not have imagined the challenges awaiting her—setting up her living space, meeting new neighbors, managing her time, learning work culture, developing new friendships, and encountering different ideas.

However, it is an unexpected tragedy that drives her to rethink all of her family's long-held traditions and beliefs. It is this soul-searching experience that challenges her to rethink the foundation of her being, and her purpose for living—the very core of her worldview. It is this testing that could bring life-changing results.

Will Eiko survive and thrive in her new life in Tokyo? Or, will the disappointments and stress lead her to escape back to the security of Sapporo? *Sky Blue* is the first book in the Sky Blue trilogy which follows Eiko's personal story of courage, adventure, and faith.

Bamboo Green: Twenty-two year old Eiko has emerged from a difficult season of physical, emotional, and spiritual trials with a stronger spirit and deeper relationship with Jesus Christ. With a positive attitude and a loving support group, Eiko contemplates her future, living and working in Tokyo.

One day, alone in a beautiful park, Eiko recalls the story of the bamboo plant. Even with no visible sign of growth for five years, a bamboo seed needs to be watered faithfully because unseen growth is taking place underground. A strong root system is forming to provide the foundation for the rapid growth that will follow, making the bamboo plant difficult to destroy. Bamboo can reach its full height and diameter in the first season. Branches and leaves form through additional seasons, as bamboo forests mature and flourish.

As the sun shines on her face, Eiko hears the Lord whisper to her, "Eiko, you are like a bamboo plant. You will mature quickly if you continue to follow Me, and I will use you to bless others." Eiko bows her head and weeps.

Bamboo Green, the third book in the Sky Blue Trilogy, follows Eiko's family, friends, and acquaintances, as she shares His love in Japan and beyond.

LIST OF JAPANESE WORDS AND ENGLISH MEANINGS

akemashite omedetou gozaimasu: New Year's greeting, said only on January 1st

arigatou: thank you

arigatou gozaimasu: formal thank you

chan: an informal title for females that goes after the person's name; includes, but not limited to, female family members, children, and same-generation friends (e.g., Mari chan)

furusato: hometown

genkan: entryway

genki: in good spirits, cheerful, energetic; o-genki (polite)

goshimpai naku: do not worry

kanji: a system of Japanese writing, using Chinese characters

gyouza: Japanese pot stickers

itadakimasu: said in unison before meals to show gratitude for the food; also a signal to start eating

ikebana: the art of Japanese flower arrangement

ishikari nabe: Hokkaido salmon hotpot, a delicious miso-based soup broth, with chunks of salmon and lots of vegetables, boiled in a clay pot on a gas burner on the table.

kadomatsu: New Year's decoration made with three things: bamboo, pine, and plum branches

kimono: traditional outer clothing, similar to a robe, worn by Japanese women, with wide sleeves and held in place with a tight sash that is tied around the middle

kun: an informal title for males that goes after the person's name; includes, but not limited to, young family members, children, juniors at work, and same-generation friends (e.g., Satoh kun)

maa-maa desu: so-so

mikan: easy-peeling Japanese citrus, similar to tangerines

miso: traditional Japanese soup, consisting of a stock called *dashi*: boiled, dried kelp (seaweed), and dried bonito (fish), into which softened miso paste (fermented soybeans) is mixed; other seasonal ingredients can be added

moshi moshi: telephone greeting, meaning "Hello. Are you there?"

nihonbare: sky blue; glorious, ideal weather, thought by Japanese to be unique to Japan. The clear sky and sun remind Japanese of their national flag.

nori: seaweed

obentou: lunchbox

ocha: green tea

odaiji ni: take care of your health

ofuro: Japanese soaking bath, filled with deep, hot water that covers your body; it requires soaping up and rinsing off outside the tub before entering

ohayou gozaimasu: good morning

oishii: delicious

onaji desu: the same

onigiri: Japanese rice balls formed into a triangular shape, often wrapped in seaweed, with a small, savory treat in the middle (fish or veggies)

onsen: natural hot springs bathing experience

otoshidama: money gift given to children in your family at New Year's

oyakodon: a Japanese dish of sauteed chicken and cooked egg in a sauce, poured over rice

samui: cold outside

san: honorific title, which goes after the person's name (i.e., Sakamoto san.)

shake: salmon

shibireru: deep, freezing cold outside (Hokkaido dialect)

soba: Japanese noodles made from buckwheat flour and usually served in a soup

taihen: awful

tatami: a type of rice straw mat, used as flooring material in traditional Japanese-style rooms

udon: a thick Japanese noodle made from wheat flour and usually served in a soup

A Recipe for Oyakodon— Chicken & Egg Rice Bowl From the Author's Husband, Tom

SHOPPING LIST

- 2 cups uncooked Boton brand Calrose rice (instant rice should not be used)
- 8 skinless chicken strips, cut into small chunks
- 1 onion, cut in half and sliced into long strips
- 2 cups Japanese dashi stock (powder sold at Asian food stores as a package of 6–8 sticks—chicken stock can be used but compromises authentic Japanese flavor)
- ¼ cup soy sauce
- 3 tablespoons *mirin* (Japanese rice wine)
- 3 tablespoons brown sugar
- 5 eggs

COOKING INSTRUCTIONS

- Cook 2 cups of Boton brand Calrose rice, per directions on rice packaging or your rice-cooker instructions.

- Place the cut up chicken in a nonstick skillet with a lid; cook and stir over medium heat until the chicken is fully cooked and beginning to brown, about 5 minutes.
- Stir in the sliced onions, and cook until the onion is soft, about 5 more minutes.
- Make dashi stock per packaging instructions.(usually 1 stick of powder per 2 cups boiling water)
- Mix soy sauce, mirin, and brown sugar into dashi stock, stirring to dissolve the sugar.
- Pour the mixture over the cooked chicken and onions.
- Bring the mixture to a boil, and let simmer until slightly reduced, about 10 minutes.
- Whisk the eggs in a bowl until well-beaten, then pour over the chicken, onions, and stock.
- Cover the skillet, reduce heat, and allow to steam for about 5 minutes, until the egg is cooked. Remove from heat.

SERVING INSTRUCTIONS

- Divide rice into 4 parts and place 1 part (¼ of cooked rice) into each of 4 deep bowls.
- Top each bowl with ¼ of the chicken and egg mixture, then spoon about ½ cup of soup into each bowl. Serves 4 people. ENJOY!

ACKNOWLEDGMENTS

There are several people I wish to thank who helped Clouds Gray reach this point. My supportive family: our grown children; and my husband, Tom, who maintains my blog at karolwhaley.com. He also agreed to my request that he share one of his favorite Japanese recipes at the end of the book for those readers who would like to try it.

I am grateful to the Lord for the many wonderful Japanese friends and acquaintances He brought into our lives, who were so kind to share not only their culture, but also their hearts with us through the years. You blessed us in so many ways and will always remain close in our hearts.

I also want to acknowledge all of the individuals and churches in the USA who felt burdened to pray for us as we learned to adjust to a culture very different from our own, and a difficult new language. We felt your prayers and saw God at work in our lives.

Clouds Gray is a work of fiction. Each one of the characters—their names and characteristics—are the product of my imagination and took on a life of their own as the story unfolded. There are two references to historical events in '93—'94, included for fun.

I owe a debt of gratitude to Kathi Macias, a gifted author of over fifty books, who edited *Clouds Gray*, as well as *Sky Blue*, the first book in the trilogy. I wish to thank Jim Hart with Hartline Literary Agency who found a path to publication and designed the covers for all three books in the Sky Blue Trilogy.

My prayer for you, the reader, is that in difficult times, as well as good, you will call out to Jesus who loves you. His grace, mercy, and hope is available to all.

Author Bio

Karol Whaley and her husband lived as Christian workers in Japan for over two decades. The Sky Blue trilogy is a work of fiction but embodies Karol's love for Christ and for the Japanese people. She and her husband, their children and grandchildren, live in southern California.

Karol hopes that you will also enjoy reading *Bamboo Green*, coming out by the end of the year. She can be contacted at jkotoba@aol.com.

IF YOU LIKED THIS BOOK, YOU MIGHT ALSO LIKE THESE BOOKS FROM OTHER HARTLINE/WHITE GLOVE AUTHORS:

Following Rain by **Darrel Nelson:** When Paul Blakely, a successful investigative reporter, visits a Seattle homeless shelter on assignment and meets Rain McKenzie, a mysterious young woman who is living with a painful past, he could never imagine the life-changing experience it will become for both of them. As he uncovers her secret, he makes an important discovery about his own life. And so begins an unexpected journey that will challenge everything they think they know about life and love.

Cinderella Texas by **Molly Noble Bull:** Opposites attract. Or do they? Alyson Spencer hoped to teach school in her beloved Dallas and didn't particularly like cowboys or a rural lifestyle. The last thing she expected to do was accept a teaching job homeschooling the children of widower, Robert Lee Greene IV called Quatro, a handsome rancher and one of the richest men in Texas. Sparks fly when daily life on his cattle ranch is not what a city-girl like Alyson expected. She is unwilling to admit that a mutual attraction has developed between her and Quatro and plans to quit her job. How can they find love and a lasting marriage when their goals in life are so different?

***The Gold Digger* by Lena Nelson Dooley:** It's 1890, and Golden, New Mexico, is a booming mining town where men far outnumber women. So when an old wealthy miner named Philip Smith finds himself in need of a nursemaid, he places an ad for a mail-order bride—despite the protests of his friend Jeremiah. Hoping to escape a perilous situation back East, young Madeleine Mercer answers the ad and arrives in town under a cloud of suspicion. But just as she begins to win over Philip—and Jeremiah himself—the secrets she left behind threaten to follow her to Golden... and tarnish her character beyond redemption.

***Christine's Promise* by Kay Moser:** Christine Boyd is the envy of all the ladies in Riverford, Texas, in 1885. She is, after all, the daughter of a revered Confederate general and the wife of a wealthy banker, Richard Boyd. Beautiful, accomplished, elegant—she exhibits the exquisite manners she was taught in antebellum Charleston. She is the perfect southern lady. Or is she? The truth is that Christine's genteel outward demeanor hides a revolutionary spirit. When she was ten years old and fleeing Union-invaded Charleston, she made a radical promise to God. She plans to keep that promise. Tradition-bound Riverford, Texas, may never be the same.

***30 Days Hath Revenge* by C. Kevin Thompson:** A Clandestine Mission. A Cryptic Message. A Chaste Promise. Blake Meyers dreamed of a peaceful end to a dutiful career with the FBI. Married now, his life was taking him in a new direction—a desk job. He would be an analyst. Ride it out until retirement. Be safe so he could enjoy family life. But when a notable member of the IRA is murdered in his London flat, Blake's secretive past propels him into the middle of an international scheme so twisted and sadistic, it will take everything Blake possesses—all of it—to save the United States from a diabolical terrorist attack. Blake Meyer Thriller: Book 1

50586130R00095

Made in the USA
San Bernardino, CA
28 June 2017